# Tales the Devil Told Me

# TALES THE DEVIL TOLD ME

## JEN FAWKES

Press 53
Winston-Salem

Press 53, LLC
PO Box 30314
Winston-Salem, NC 27130

First Edition

Library of Congress Control Number
2021931380

Printed on acid-free paper
ISBN 978-1-950413-32-4

For my mother, Julie
You should have been a Queen

"The devil told you that, the devil told you!" the little man screamed, and in his rage he stamped his right foot so hard that it went into the ground right up to his waist. Then in his fury he seized his left foot with both hands and tore himself in two.

—"Rumpelstiltskin"

The author wishes to thank the editors of the following literary journals, in which versions of these stories first appeared:

*Day One*: "Tigers Don't Apologize"

*Jersey Devil Press*: "Dynamics"

*The Massachusetts Review*: "Demerol, Demerol, Benzedrine, Schnaps"

*Michigan Quarterly Review*: "Never, Never"

*Mid-American Review*: "Tiny Bones"

*The Pinch*: "As You Can Imagine, This Makes Dating Difficult"

*The Southeast Review*: "Dear Ahab"

*Tampa Review*: "A Moment on the Lips"

# CONTENTS

# DEMEROL, DEMEROL, BENZEDRINE, SCHNAPS

There was one cure for what ailed the rumpelstilt, and that cure was baby. Bouncing, drooling, clinging human baby. Unlike the rest of his miniscule race, the rumpelstilt had been born with a surfeit of affection and no one upon whom to bestow it. He'd tried foisting his love onto infants he'd sired during the spring rutting season, but once expelled from the womb, his kind are capable of locomotion and independent thought, and when the rumpelstilt attempted to cuddle his children, they begged him to stop suffocating them and let them get on with their lives. More than one bit him. So the rumpelstilt, who had no flair for mischief, who unlike his brethren felt no scorn for humans and was no good at frightening them, decided the only way to satisfy his lust for reciprocated affection was to get his tiny hands on a human child.

In front of his cottage, which stood beside a mountain at the forest's end, the rumpelstilt drank Kentucky bourbon whiskey, danced around the fire, and plotted. The world was teeming with cast-off human young—this he knew—but he did not want just any child. Walls and doors were no impediment to the rumpelstilt, and he could circumnavigate the globe before you or I could say *jackrabbit*, and he was well aware of the multitudinous crowds of children whose parents could not or would not care for them. Children of the incarcerated or the poverty-stricken or the addled or the melancholy. Children who'd lost their parents to car accidents or intestinal parasites. Children who, in addition to being alone in the great universe, were themselves sick or maimed or otherwise incapacitated. When he looked at them, the rumpelstilt was overwhelmed by the intensity of their need. He was also slightly disgusted. Their hollow eyes and snotty noses and trembling lips struck him as maudlin and oppressive. The rumpelstilt preferred healthy, whole children, children whose parents would willingly give their own lives to save them. "I must find myself such a child!" he cried as he emptied the bottle of bourbon and flung it into the fire. The glass shattered, and sparks billowed skyward. The rumpelstilt stumbled, falling on his face. He was beginning to suspect that he had a drinking problem, but he was sure the inherent responsibility of childrearing would pull him out of his downward spiral.

Eight months after he'd come across the girl weeping in a bar called The Waxwing Slain, the rumpelstilt stood on the sidewalk outside a hospital, nursing a mezcal hangover, unable to recall whether or not he'd eaten the worm. The girl had roomy, childbearing hips, and she'd promised him her firstborn in exchange for his assistance; they'd sealed the deal with sixteen-year-old single malt scotch. In the ensuing months, the rumpelstilt had stocked his cottage with diapers and stuffed toys and rubber-nippled bottles, with a playpen and jammies and formula and baby powder, with a contraption called a Jolly Jumper that allowed a harnessed infant to bounce to his heart's content at the end of a tether. The rumpelstilt had pored over parenting magazines and books on childcare, and he was certain that he'd forgotten nothing. Now, as he gazed through automatic glass doors into the hospital—where scrub-clad residents and nurses and technicians streamed with purposeful efficiency, reminding him of ancient rivers that, over time, had hollowed out great mountains—his head throbbed. His eyes twitched. Mezcal sweat rolled down his back. He was about to meet his baby—the vessel into which he would pour the love that had been accruing in his tiny breast for three hundred years—and he was flooded with a maniacal sense of joy.

"Holy shit," the girl said when the rumpelstilt appeared in the maternity ward waiting area. "I thought you were a figment of my imagination."

He shook his head. "You've given birth."

The girl, whose blonde hair was piled like an unruly magpie's nest on top of her head, whose eyes were glassy, who wore sweatpants, nodded. "How did you know?"

The rumpelstilt shrugged. He knew she'd given birth the same way he knew the ancient, spotty woman seated to the girl's left had eaten tuna salad and tapioca pudding for lunch, the same way he knew that on a nearby stretch of I-95, a speeding convertible was about to clip a tractor-trailer while changing lanes, causing a multi-car pileup that would stop traffic for the rest of the afternoon. "I guess you know why I'm here," he said.

The girl closed her eyes. She held up a finger. "Give me a minute."

In the recesses of her brain, she sought the memory of her meeting with the rumpelstilt. Perhaps she should have told Dr. Schmidt of her addictive tendencies when he offered her something for the pain, but she *had* been in pain—actual physical pain—after giving birth six weeks before her due date. And ever since, she'd been in severe emotional pain—or maybe she'd been in such pain before the birth—but now, Demerol stood like a soft, feathery barrier between her and discomfort. What was she supposed to be remembering? Oh yes, the tiny man who'd approached her eight months earlier in The Waxwing Slain. She'd been drinking scotch, and he'd asked why she was crying, and instead of telling him about Dale and Riley, she'd spun a line of bullshit about a king who wouldn't marry her unless she first proved she could spin straw into gold. The rumpelstilt was no bigger than Riley had been at two, when he'd fit perfectly into her arms, and she'd been sorely tempted to pick up the little man and cradle him, to rock him, to press her cheek to his and say "shh"

and "there now," but she'd known this would only piss him
off. In spite of his size, the rumpelstilt was clearly full-grown,
and grown men only like being babied in private. It turned
out that he could really hold his liquor, and after a hazy series
of misadventures, they'd ended up back at her place with a
quantity of straw and a spinning wheel. The next morning,
her apartment was stocked with bright threads of 24-karat
gold, and there was no sign of the rumpelstilt. Where had
they come up with a spinning wheel? Had they slept together? Jesus, had she fucked this homunculus? The girl knew
she'd promised him something in exchange for the gold—
something that, in addition to making her seem like a monster, was impossible for her to give.

"Where is your husband?" the little man said, his
bright eyes roaming the waiting area. "Is he prepared to
give me the child?"

"Maybe you should have a seat," the girl said, tapping
the chair beside her. The Demerol was making her feel char-
itable and empathetic; it was also making her yearn to slow
dance with a tall, bearded man. Part of her wanted to confess her lies to the rumpelstilt, not just the story of the king
and the straw and the gold, not just the fact that her firstborn was a four-year-old now living in the desert South-
west with his father—who'd won full custody by having
her declared unfit—but lies she had not yet told him and
those she regularly told herself. As he hopped onto the
chair, however, as he launched into a diatribe about his
burning desire for a child, she knew she couldn't bear to
pull the rug out from under him. His words reminded her
of the way she herself had felt in the early days of her
marriage. Before she'd had Riley. When she'd thought giving birth could change her. When she'd imagined her child
would act as a sieve—collecting her faults and shortcomings. That he would distill her, eliminating her yen for Per-
cocets and chilled shots of Jagermeister, her inability to
cook a decent meal, the things that convinced Dale she
was crazy. She'd thought Riley's birth would be a cata-
lyst, transforming her into the woman she should have

been all along. Tractable. Decent. Normal. Her son was an undeniable gift, but when he turned three, the girl was struck by the unbearable certainty that she was the same person she'd always been. That change is impossible. That beneath the surface, life is a black void—a sucking vortex against which we struggle pointlessly. She'd been bathing Riley at the time, and when Dale walked into the house that night, he found her folded into the small cabinet beneath the bathroom sink. Every television and radio in the house was blaring. Doors and windows were thrown open despite the February freeze. Riley lay curled, naked and shivering, in the middle of the living room rug.

"Things will be different once I bring home the child," said the rumpelstilt as a young resident entered the maternity ward waiting area and strode toward them. "They must be."

The girl tried to pass off the tiny man as a third cousin—a native of New Guinea—but Dr. Schmidt had grown up in the forests of Bavaria, and though he was piloting a Benzedrine-fueled rocket into the thirtieth hour of a thirty-six-hour shift, he knew a rumpelstilt when he saw one. The creatures had haunted the cottage of his grandparents, who'd raised him after his father was buried beneath an avalanche of deceptively feathery-looking snow while attempting to scale the Matterhorn, and his mother crawled into a bottle of Schnaps. From then on, Dr. Schmidt caught only rare glimpses of his *Mutti*, slumped in front of the ale house. "Fie," his grandmother would say, dragging him toward the market, avoiding the hollow blue eyes of her daughter, but the boy could not turn away from his mother's gaze. According to his grandmother, Schnaps was manufactured by the devil, and she kept it around the cottage for one reason only—to catch rumpelstilts, who could not resist it. At night, she would set out large bowls of the liquor, and the boy often woke to the sound of surprisingly robust singing. Sitting up, he would discover a drunken rumpelstilt stumbling across the foot of his bed. His grandmother would bind the incapacitated creature and carry him to the woodpile behind the cottage. "If you let them go, they just keep coming back," she would say in response to her grandson's protestations as she hoisted the great axe over her head, as she swung it down and into the tree stump, cleaving the rumpelstilt neatly in two. The boy watched her dispatch hundreds of the creatures in this fashion, and though he usually wept, the sight of the rumpelstilt halves rising briefly to hop on one foot always cheered him.

He hadn't seen a rumpelstilt since he'd left Bavaria for the rapturous rigors of Yale Medical School, but a rumpelstilt was definitely sitting beside the girl who'd given birth to the as-yet-unnamed premature infant in incubator seven of the Neonatal Intensive Care Unit. Dr. Schmidt found this girl tragically beautiful, and he'd been struggling with the desire to rescue her from herself and from the cold world. Benzedrine gave him a godlike sense of omniscience, and he was certain that beneath her unwashed, glassy exterior, the girl was as pure as the mountainous snow that had buried his *Vati* under the Matternhorn. He was also certain that the rumpelstilt was menacing her, and a surge of protective feeling welled up in his broad Bavarian breast.

"I'm afraid we are not yet out of the woods," Dr. Schmidt said, wishing the words didn't sound so rehearsed and recitative. "Your son still is not producing the agent that helps prevent his lungs from collapsing. We are giving him supplemental oxygen, but we do not know when he will be able to breathe on his own. When a premature newborn stays on a respirator too long, other complications can arise, and we have to be vigilant about infection. But he is a tough little guy, and we are doing absolutely everything that can be done."

At the sight of the strapping Nordic doctor, instinctual ire had risen in the rumpelstilt. It was what the man said, however, that shook him to his foundation. Something was wrong with the child. *His* child. The rumpelstilt didn't understand how the boy's premature birth had escaped his apprehension. He'd always thought of himself as omniscient, but now wondered if he might have a blind spot or two. After dropping his bombshell, squeezing the girl's shoulders for too long, and eyeing the rumpelstilt with suspicion, the blond doctor buzzed from the waiting area like a tightly wound clockwork soldier. The rumpelstilt's hands trembled, and he wished he'd brought along the whiskey flask that fit so perfectly into his tiny pocket. He turned to the girl, who blinked at him, a look of concern smeared over her face.

"Is there a bar?" he said.

"In the hospital?" She shook her head. "No."

"There should be."

"You're probably right."

"What happened?"

"He came too soon," she said. "His lungs aren't fully developed."

"But eventually, he'll be all right. Premature infants don't usually die."

The girl shrugged. "He's not yet out of the woods."

"Is it possible for me to see him?"

She studied the blue tile beneath her feet. "If you'd like."

Even the hospital's smallest masks and gowns and gloves and booties were far too big for the rumpelstilt. Once she'd donned her own protective gear, the girl wrapped a pink gown around him until only his bright eyes were visible. Cradling him like an infant, she carried him into the NICU. In the deathly quiet room, she approached an incubator—one of a flock that stood on tall stands. Inside the clear plastic box, illuminated by a warm overhanging light, lay a child nearly as small as the infants the rumpelstilt had fathered—children who'd rejected his affection before he'd had a chance to offer it. The boy looked nothing like a healthy newborn. He was far too skinny, and his skin was red and ill-fitting. Tubes and wires tethering him to machines sprouted from his mouth and navel, wrists and ankles, chest and belly. A white cap covered his head. His wrinkled chest inflated and deflated weakly. The rumpelstilt expected to feel overwhelmed by the unease that normally descended on him at the sight of damaged children. Instead, longing surged through him, tearing a sob from his throat.

"Shh," the girl said. "There now." Holding the rumpelstilt reminded her of cradling Riley; in place of the sweet
fragrance that had risen continuously from her son, however, was the sour smell of sweat and mezcal. But if she
closed her eyes and held her breath, she was able to imagine that she held her child. Bouncing the tiny man up and
down, she hummed into his ear.

"Why haven't you named him?" the rumpelstilt said.

The girl didn't answer; she kept humming and jiggling,
swaying from side to side.

"Where is your husband?" the rumpelstilt said, and even
as he said it, he understood that the girl had no husband.
That there had never been a king who demanded she spin
straw into gold. She had, instead, spun for the rumpelstilt
a fairy story, and he'd been blind and desperate and drunk
enough to fall for it. He'd picked the girl up in a bar, and
she was probably of questionable character. He'd allowed
himself to be hoodwinked. He'd spun straw into gold for
no reason, and he'd spent the last eight months waiting
and preparing and childproofing his cottage for a damaged
infant. The girl had probably caused the baby's premature
birth with her irresponsible behavior. She was probably
hoping for its death. The rumpelstilt wanted to leap from
her arms and flee, but she'd wrapped him as tightly as a spi-
der wraps a fly, and he found himself at her mercy.

"Let me go." The rumpelstilt knew it was within his
power to free himself, but struggle as he might, he found
that he could not. "Please."

"Shh," said the girl. "There now."

Released from their protective gear, the rumpelstilt and the
girl took the elevator to the lobby and wandered through the
automatic glass doors. She hadn't left the hospital since she'd
given birth five days earlier, and excitement percolated in the
girl at the sight of the outside world. The day had been long
and hazy, and the declining sun washed the sky in bands of
pink and orange. Affection for the rumpelstilt mounted within her, and she wondered how she would feel about walking
down the street with the tiny man, about ducking with him

into a tavern that hadn't changed its décor or personnel in forty years, had she not been cradled in the soft bosom of Demerol. Embarrassed, probably. Ashamed. But painkillers are almost as effective as alcohol in the abolition of shame. After Dale took Riley away—after he put nearly two thousand miles between the girl and her son—she'd gone to a different bar every night, determined to shed her modesty. She couldn't recall every man she'd met during those months, nor did she want to. They'd all screwed her, but only one had fathered the tiny, wrinkled infant languishing in an incubator in the NICU. And only one had provided her with the means to indefinitely pay her rent and bills.

"I never got to thank you for the gold," she said.

The rumpelstilt ordered a double bourbon. He drained half the highball in one gulp. "Don't mention it."

"If the baby lives," the girl said, "I'm glad you'll be the one raising him."

"Doesn't it hurt? The thought of giving him up?"

Having taken a Demerol not thirty minutes before, just then she felt no pain, but the girl nodded. "Sometimes you give up children," she said. "You do it for their own good."

He hadn't cradled or bottle-fed or burped any of the hundreds of rumpelstilts he'd fathered over the course of his interminable life; he hadn't taught a single boy to shave or given away as brides any of the girls, yet the rumpelstilt had named them all. Using these designators, he was able to call up each of their faces, and he liked to imagine that in time, all his children would come together. That there would arise some holiday or occasion on which they would sit down and exchange words of affection and appreciation. This fantasy had sustained the rumpelstilt during many sleepless nights, but over the years, it had become increasingly difficult to buy into, and he'd discovered that liquor aided greatly in the suspension of his disbelief. In truth, none of his children would have recognized him, and this was as it should be. If they hadn't yet been cleaved in two by stout Bavarian housewives, each of them was doing exactly what he or she was born to do. Haunting humans. Rutting in the spring. Getting on with their lives.

"What about Caspar?" he said. "Or Melchior? Or Balthazar?"

The girl gave him a puzzled look.

"For the baby," the rumpelstilt said. Cocooned in the creeping comfort of bourbon, he studied the girl, who looked, in the dingy tavern light, like a fairy princess or a queen. "We should settle on a name."

Back in the maternity ward waiting area, the girl dozed on a blue chair, but the rumpelstilt was restless. He roamed the halls of the hospital, running through the names he'd given his male offspring, searching for one that would suit the baby. This would be the first name he bestowed that would be recognized by its recipient, and he wanted to get it right. He thought about Shortribs, Sheepshanks, or Laceleg, but these were too bizarre. He thought about Conrad or Harry, but these were too run-of-the-mill. After making a circuit of the building, the rumpelstilt returned to the maternity ward. In front of the broad silver doors leading into the NICU, he nearly tumbled into a rectangular plastic basin from which wafted the unmistakable scent of Schnaps. The rumpelstilt stooped over the basin and closed his eyes, inhaling deeply. He couldn't remember the last time he'd drunk the fruit-based liquor, and in spite of his very recent decision to reduce his alcohol intake, he didn't see the harm in having a taste.

"Drink up, little rumpelstilt," whispered Dr. Schmidt, who crouched nearby, watching the tiny man lap from the basin. At the end of his thirty-six-hour shift, the resident had driven home, showered, stopped at a liquor store and then a hardware store, and returned to the hospital. He'd placed the Schnaps-filled basin in front of the NICU and secreted himself in a dim exam room from which he commanded a clear view of his distilled bait. Still flying on Benzedrine, he thought about how grateful the girl would be. He imagined that once she was free of the rumpelstilt, she would pledge herself to him. That she would tear off her sweatpants and stained T-shirt, let down her hair, wrap her arms around him. He'd been crouching in the exam room for two hours, stroking the handle of his brand-new axe, when the rumpelstilt appeared in the corridor.

Dr. Schmidt's heart galloped. His brain rattled. His blood thrummed through his branching blue veins. He was a Teutonic Warrior. A Wagnerian Viking. A Great War Eagle circling his prey. He could hear the night nurse clear her throat at the desk three floors below. He sensed the passing of an elderly man in the burn ward. Dr. Schmidt's nose was full of the commingled scents of blood and feces and urine and pus, but he did not choke. Instead, the malodorous scents sustained him, fueling his mastery, his fury. The rumpelstilt drained the basin, and once the creature was weaving across the corridor, conducting an invisible orchestra and hiccupping and singing an off-key song about baking and brewing and a child and the significance of a name, Dr. Schmidt crept from his hiding place. He was the shadow. The resurrection and the life. A regular *Ubermensch*. He was able to put Humpty Dumpty back together again, and it was his duty to dispatch this rumpelstilt as his grandmother would have done, as his sad-eyed mother might have commanded if she hadn't abandoned him for Schnaps and sorrow. He was a panther, a puma, a Germanic jaguar, and as he crept up on the little man, he found that his feet had been transformed into velvet paws. He no longer needed to breathe.

"Tomorrow, I quit cold turkey!" the rumpelstilt cried into the dead silence of the hospital corridor. He rode waves of Schnaps toward the NICU. He lifted a hand, and the double doors yawned open. The perfect name was stuck in his throat, and he thought another look at the baby would jar it loose. Inside the dim room, he shimmied up the stand to incubator number seven. He studied the slumbering infant inside the plastic box—so small, so fragile, so clearly in need. The child's fingers clenched and unclenched. His wrinkled chest rose and fell with the imposed rhythm of the respirator, its white hose taped into his mouth. The rumpelstilt squinted, and in the child's minute face, he saw echoes of the girl. As they'd walked from the tavern to the hospital, the rumpelstilt had explained to her how to find his cottage, beside the mountain at the forest's end. He'd described the sun that did not set until it was commanded, edging every leaf and branch and bud with gold, washing the wood in blinding brilliance. He'd described the creeping mists of spring, how they coiled around legs and tree trunks, hiding the leaf-strewn ground from view. He'd told her about the countless creatures that visited his cottage—deer and squirrels and foxes, yes, but also ibexes and capybaras and rhinoceroses. Like his brethren, the rumpelstilt had always lived in solitude. He'd been preparing his tidy, lonely world for the baby for eight months, but he did not expect to be struck, as he walked beside the girl through gathering dusk, by the unshakable conviction that she should accompany her child. She'd been born to dwell in his cottage, and they could do more for the baby together than they ever could separately. And for each other. The rumpelstilt wasn't normally attracted to humans, but there was something about the girl. He sensed that they suffered from a similar ailment. That she was as forsaken as he. Before she'd fallen asleep in the waiting area, the rumpelstilt had introduced the topic of their cohabitation. She'd smiled, promising to give him an answer when she woke.

"You should not be here. You will infect the premature infants."

The rumpelstilt lifted his head to find Dr. Schmidt looming over him like Mount Zugspitze, the highest peak in the Bavarian Alps. The square-jawed resident snatched the rumpelstilt from the incubator and dangled the tiny man by one foot in front of him.

"That's my baby," the rumpelstilt said, his words slurred. Upside down, he'd lost his bearings, but he tried to point toward incubator number seven. "That's my child."

"If you have a god, rumpelstilt," Dr. Schmidt said, "I suggest that you pray to him."

The doctor stalked the hospital corridors, clutching the inverted rumpelstilt in one hand and babbling about his Bavarian boyhood, about his father dying under the Matterhorn, about his mother's sorrowful eyes, about his grandmother's unquenchable thirst for the blood of rumpelstilts.

For emphasis, he brandished his axe. "You don't have to do this," the rumpelstilt kept saying. "I have so much love to give." In an operating theatre, Dr. Schmidt strapped the little man to a stainless steel table. "I could have borrowed a saw from the morgue," he said, hefting the axe over his head, "but I am a sucker for tradition."

The shiny blade seemed to whistle through the air for hours. During its descent, the rumpelstilt grew painfully sober. He wondered about his yen for a human baby, whether it might have been selfish in nature. Something sinister merely masquerading as love. He had a vision of the barefoot girl standing in front of his cottage, wearing a blue dress. Braced against her hip was a child, a small boy with reddish curls and pink cheeks. The girl pointed out a cedar waxwing, trilling in a flowering ash, and the boy clapped his hands. "Timothy!" the rumpelstilt cried just before the axe bit into him, cleaving him neatly in two.

Once the baby's lungs had strengthened, once he'd gained weight and grown into his skin, the girl took her son and fled the hospital. Three weeks had passed since she'd woken in the maternity ward waiting area, an echoing cry humming through her, certain that she should name the boy Timothy. A moment later, Dr. Schmidt had appeared, grinning maniacally and clutching the halved remains of the rumpelstilt. The girl's Demerol barrier crumbled; she fell to her knees and yowled like a wounded animal, releasing sorrow she'd never released for Riley, or for premature Timothy. Once the Bavarian doctor understood that the rumpelstilt had not been menacing her, he apologized profusely, but she would never forgive him. She wrapped the rumpelstilt halves in a hospital gown and placed them in a Styrofoam ice chest. She followed the little man's directions to the cottage next to the mountain at the forest's end, where she found things just as he'd described them. She settled into a new life there, certain that this was the circumstance in which she was meant to dwell.

After the cathartic release brought on by the rumpelstilt's death, the girl found that she had no more use for Demerol.

She'd dedicated a large portion of her life to the avoidance of pain, but now she found exquisite beauty in discomfort. She'd never been so vividly in touch with the workings of her body, never so aware of the blood in her veins. She embraced her fear of motherhood; she clutched it to her breast and wrestled it to the ground. She rocked Timothy and whispered "shh" and "there now." She buckled him into the Jolly Jumper and watched him bounce for hours. She learned to accept his faults and shortcomings as she learned to accept her own. She encouraged him to open himself to love, to fear, to pain, to shame. She dreamed that someday he would meet his brother, that they would come together to exchange words of affection and appreciation. She took him for long rambles in the forest, naming hydrangea and forsythia, honeycreeper and nuthatch, silver poplar and black walnut. When the boy was old enough to ask about his father, she would direct him to the unmarked white stone south of the cottage—the stone under which she'd buried the rumpelstilt's remains. Sleep would often elude the girl, and she would creep from the cottage to curl her body around this stone. Pressing her face into the earth, allowing darkness to wash over and through her, she would resurrect the rumpelstilt, who would assure her that she was not alone.

## AS YOU CAN IMAGINE, THIS MAKES DATING DIFFICULT

The burlap sack wasn't the first thing he noticed. It covered her head completely, but she stood in the shadows, and he'd had a few before he came in. He settled on a stool with his back to the bar, his eyes skimming the dance floor. Music pounded the brick walls, the low-slung ceiling, but her voice sliced through the din like piano wire through a windpipe.

"How may I serve you?"

It wasn't the words but the way her tongue cradled them and thrust them through her teeth. Though she stood on the business side of the bar—though they were separated by three feet of battered teak—he could have sworn she'd spoken directly into his ear.

"Beer," he said. "Whatever's on tap."

He didn't bring up the writhing burlap sack, and neither did she. He sat on the stool until night was washed away by dawn, until the overheads blazed and the barback finished mopping. By then, he knew she'd grown up far away, a place she described as *the edge of the world*. She had two sisters, both younger. Her parents were monsters. She'd been in town less than a year. "My band is performing tonight," she said, scrubbing pint glasses in the metal bar sink. "Perhaps you would like to come?"

He smiled. That sounded like fun.

She stooped over the sink, and the sack's surface twitched and bubbled. He wondered what had happened to her face. Car accident? Jealous boyfriend? Acid or box cutter or lye? What he could see of her body—draped in fabric tied over one shoulder and cinched with rope at the waist—was extraordinary. Slender arms, angular shoulders, pearly expanse of skin interrupted by wing-shaped clavicle. He studied the perfectly formed breasts nestled beneath cream-colored cloth, tried to discern which of his colleagues might have done them. Dr. Lovejoy, he decided, or possibly Dr. Rubenstein.

"That is that," she said, emerging from behind the bar with a messenger bag and a bottle of water. He saw now that her garment fell to the floor, covering her feet entirely. As she moved toward him, seeming to glide rather than step, he finally noticed that the burlap sack had no eyeholes. "Let us go."

Outside, a yellow rim of sun glanced over the horizon. He hailed a cab and helped her inside. He pressed a crumpled wad of bills into the driver's hand and instructed the man to take her wherever she wanted to go.

"I hope to see you tonight," she said, thrusting the sack through the open window. "It is next to impossible to meet someone in this town."

Strengthening light poured across streets, spilled over grass, splashed up buildings, soaked filthy sidewalks, pooled on corners. In the cloudless blue sky, he saw the wing-shaped clavicle nestled between her throat and chest, imagined it taking flight.

That morning, he did a brow lift and a tummy tuck. He vacuumed belly and thigh fat out of three different women. In the afternoon, he sat on the brown couch of Dr. Lana Radcliff, who perched opposite him on a blue chair. Her office was located three floors below his, and he'd been seeing her weekly for almost a year.

"Are you sleeping?"

He shook his head.

She turned, reaching across the desk behind her for a

prescription pad. "I know you don't like pills, but some-times knowing they're there can help." She tore the paper free and passed it across the void. She blinked. She smiled. "How's the other thing?"

The other thing was the reason he'd started seeing Lana—his compulsion to critique every woman he encoun-tered and, with a mental scalpel, modify the parts of her he deemed less than ideal. Though this made him very good at his job, his inability to turn it off bothered him. Faces and bodies were weighed and dissected. Dotted lines only he could see materialized on skin, marks indicating what should be tucked, sucked, or lifted. The woman behind the deli counter. The woman who delivered his mail. Dr. Lana Radcliff.

"Things haven't really improved," he said.

"Have you been doing the exercise?"

The exercise involved looking in the mirror nightly and telling himself that people were just as the divine power of the universe made them, that he was merely a man, that he had no right to judge others. In time, Lana believed this recitation would open his *chakras* and unblock his *qi* flow, freeing him from negative obsessions.

"I have," he said, and dotted lines appeared on Lana's face. His mind made the incisions: thinned her cheeks, built up her chin, streamlined her nose, plumped her lips. Her long, graying hair was colored and styled, her breasts inflated, her glasses replaced by contacts, the shapeless sweater and slacks that wrapped her thin figure torn away. He wondered if, as they sat chatting on Thursday after-noons, she ever considered the ways in which he amended her. "But it doesn't seem to be helping."

Lana nodded. "Keep trying, Mitchell. Transformation takes time. And effort. You have to really want to change."

He studied his long, tapered fingers. "I met someone."

Lana blinked. She smiled.

"I told her I'd come see her band tonight."

"Good!"

"I also told her I sell insurance."

Lana propped her chin on a fist. "Why lie?"

"She was wearing a burlap sack over her head. I thought my profession might bother her."

"Why was she wearing the sack?"

"I assume something happened to her face."

Lana leaned forward. "What's the attraction?"

"She's got a great voice. And a great body. She's easy to talk to."

Lana blinked. She smiled.

"And there's the sack."

"Eventually you'll have to come to terms with what's under the sack, Mitchell."

They were called The Gorgons, and when he walked into the cramped, dingy club, they'd just taken the stage. She wore the same draping garment she'd had on when he met her, or maybe she had one for every day of the week. He ordered a beer and stood at the back of the room. Studying the kids who packed the place, he wondered about her age. The night before, he'd gotten the strange sense that she'd been around since long before his birth. Ridiculous, of course.

She still wore the burlap sack, and shifting, multicolored lights played over it, exaggerating its movement. Two back-up singers wearing similar sacks and dresses flanked her, and when he realized the sack was a gimmick—part of the show—he felt slightly crushed. The rest of the band stood in shadow toward the back of the stage. The droning, weaving music that spilled from their instruments seemed to project patterns into the smoky air. Her voice—ethereal, otherworldly—slid between notes. It twined around chords. The audience stood body to body, but he thought she sang for him alone. When the set ended, she left the stage and snaked through the crowd.

"Mitchell." She was out of breath. "I am so glad you came."

The backup singers turned out to be her sisters, and after introducing them, she led him to a booth across the room from the stage. They settled opposite one another on cracked turquoise vinyl. "So," she said, "what did you think?"

"It was great." He reached across the table to touch her folded hands. "You were great."

"I appreciate the compliment."

He studied the sack's movements. Parts of it roiled like a storm-tossed sea. Others convulsed spasmodically.

"You are wondering about the sack."

"No," he said. "Not in the least."

"Of course you are. And I cannot blame you."

Another band had taken the stage—a drum and guitar duo made up of twin girls with stringy white-blonde hair. Their melodies reminded him of amusement parks and surf movies.

"Years ago," she said, "my beauty was transformed into something terrible. Now any man who gazes upon me forfeits his life."

Hope glimmered within him. "It's not a gimmick then."

She shook the sack, which rustled softly. "If I did not cover my face, the members of our audience would turn to stone."

He knew he should feel cheated, swindled, as though the world were diminishing. Instead, he sensed a thousand doors opening.

"I understand if you want to leave. This is the point at which most men do."

The white-blonde twins were in the middle of a slow number. He stood and extended a hand. Later, when the tempo of the music increased, they continued dancing cheek to burlap. The churning and rippling of the rough sack against his face and neck felt like a hundred simultaneous caresses.

The sack made it easier for him to hack and slice through his day, to clip and tuck and suck, to scrape and abrade, to flatter and wheedle and assure. When he caught sight of her waiting outside his building after work, or standing in the doorframe of the apartment she shared with her sisters, or lying naked beside him on his king-sized bed or her futon in the light of dawn, he was confronted not with a chin or a cheek or an eyebrow but with the blank, unmarked surface of the sack, and this pleased him endlessly.

He missed three sessions with Dr. Lana Radcliff. He gave up the exercise; he stopped telling himself that people were as the divine power of the universe made them, that he had no right to judge others, that he was just a man. He took on new patients and packed his day with procedures. In the streets, in restaurants, he mentally rearranged women and handed them his card. Because she was waiting for him at the end of the day—featureless and obscure, impossible to correct—his compulsion no longer bothered him.

Then he saw her without the sack.

One morning after he'd left her apartment, he discovered that he'd forgotten his wallet. He found her standing naked and sackless in front of the cracked mirror over her dresser. In the glass, a slithering mass of serpents encircled her head. Some hissed and struck with lightning speed at empty air; others undulated slowly, forked tongues flicking. Scales glinted and sparked in the rays of the morning sun—a hypnotic melding of hues. He was no expert, but he felt certain that no two of the snakes were alike.

The serpentine cloud framed a face—one he never could have imagined. It was the most well-proportioned face he'd ever seen, and it projected shock and horror. The symmetry of its features convinced him that it had been measured and laid out by the divine power of the universe. Gazing upon it, he was flooded with the same giddy elation that had coursed through him as a boy when, after losing his mother in a crowded department store, he'd found himself back in her arms.

But in the mirror, the smooth forehead creased; the straight nose wrinkled; the plump lips pouted. Two pools of clear cerulean blinked in frustration. "I thought you had gone!" Her voice was anguished.

"You're divine."

He moved forward, and in the mirror, she lifted a hand. "You must not come closer!"

"Why not?"

"If I turn around, you will die."

She plucked the burlap sack from the cluttered dresser

and maneuvered it over the hissing serpents until the face in the mirror was veiled once more.

"I don't understand," he said.

She pulled on a robe, sat on the bed and sighed. "I did not tell you it is possible to gaze upon my reflection because I know what it has done to men in the past. You seemed content with the sack, and I hoped we could go on this way indefinitely. It was foolish, but I could not help myself. I like you very much."

He studied the rough, swelling surface of the sack, once a canvas onto which he could paint any image or, as he preferred, no image at all. Now, he saw only the face he'd glimpsed in the mirror.

"I must be honest with you, Mitchell. I am not proud of this, but for many years, I took my anger out on others. I did not cover my face; I directed its terrible power at people intentionally. In this way I hoped to take revenge for my cursed existence."

Dazed, he sat down beside her, and she took his hand.

"Eventually I grew weary of that life. No matter what had been done to me, I did not have to live at the edge of the world. I did not have to hurt others because I'd been hurt. My sisters and I left our dark, dreary home, and I found music, the thing about which I am most passionate."

He had a full day of procedures scheduled. Rhinoplasty, brow lift, cheek implants, mentoplasty, facelift. Now that he'd seen her face, however, he couldn't go through with any of them. He could never approximate the beauty to which he'd borne witness.

"Is there a way to reverse what was done to you?"

She shook the sack, which swished and crinkled.

"Have you consulted a cosmetic surgeon?"

"There is nothing wrong with the surface of my face. It is something deeper. One cannot access it with knives."

"We could try."

"We?"

He dropped to his knees before her. "I don't sell insurance. I'm a plastic surgeon. Maybe there's something I can do."

"Why did you lie, Mitchell?" Anguish crept back into her voice.

"I thought you might be put off by my profession."

She stood and walked to the window. When she turned, sunshine coursed around the twitching sack, edging it with light. "This is why I hoped you would never see my reflection. It changes things. You will always yearn to display my face. But I will wear the sack for as long as I live. I have come to terms with that."

"Surely something can be done . . ."

This time, as she shook it, the sack trilled loudly. "There is no fixing me. In this situation, you are powerless."

"But . . ."

"No." She pointed to the door. "I think you should go."

He shut down his practice and spent eight months backpacking through Brazil and Ecuador. With a group of native scientists and volunteers, he catalogued flora and fauna, studying mankind's impact on the rainforests, surrounding himself with examples of rare beauty—macaws and emerald tree frogs and plants that produce a single, exquisite bloom only once in a human lifetime. Upon his return, he made an appointment with Dr. Lana Radcliff, and when he entered her office, he was dumbfounded by her metamorphosis. She'd had her nose, lips, cheeks, and chin done. She'd replaced her glasses with jade contact lenses. Her hair had been darkened and cut into flattering layers. She wore a short skirt, strappy heels, and a sweater that hugged her new breasts. "Well?" she said. "What do you think?"

He didn't know how to respond. The sight of her— hacked and molded into one surgeon's notion of beauty — brought everything back. The face he'd gone away to forget. The abject hopelessness that had swept over him after he'd glimpsed it, a feeling in which he'd very nearly drowned.

"I've been saving up for years." Though her mouth was unfamiliar, though her eyes were all wrong, Lana still blinked. Still smiled. "It's changed my life."

"Good." His gaze skipped around the office, alighting

on things then winging away. The lamp, her nose, the desk, her chin, the framed portrait of galloping wild horses, her breasts. "I'm happy for you."

"How was your trip? Were you able to get things into perspective?"

After he'd seen the face in the cracked mirror, Mitchell had lost his touch for cosmetic surgery. The guiding lines had vanished. Unable to determine what to tuck and what to lift, he'd had no idea where to make the first cut. He'd hoped his sojourn in the jungle would refresh him. That the beauty of the natural world would seep into him, giving him a new perspective on the modification of women. When he was confronted with the remodeled Lana Radcliff, however, he knew he would never perform another procedure.

"Mitchell?" Lana blinked. She smiled. "What's on your mind?"

"I don't think I can reopen my practice."

She tented her manicured fingers. "Is this about what was under the sack?"

He nodded.

"What if I give you an exercise? Something to recite in the mirror each night? Something like, 'Beauty is subjective. There is no ideal form. The face I saw was an illusion. Whether she's as the divine power of the universe made her or surgically enhanced, every woman is beautiful in her own way'?"

"Maybe." He let his eyes linger on Lana's new face. "Do you believe that?"

She uncrossed her legs. She leaned forward and embraced her pert breasts. She smiled. She blinked. "It's not about what I believe, Mitchell. It's about what works for you."

For nearly a month, he recited the words. When he woke in the night, he took long jaunts through empty streets—streets that bore no resemblance to their daytime counterparts. He chanted the words while walking and in the shower and at the gym. They became a mantra, one that flowed into and out of his consciousness steadily, and he achieved a state of mind in which he could almost believe them.

He was considering reopening his practice when he
spied her on the street. Her cinched garment brushed
the cement as she floated ahead of him. The back of the
burlap sack swelled and trembled. He shut his eyes, but
when he looked again, she was still there. Compelled
to catch her, he quickened his pace. Once he was close
enough to discern the rustling of the sack, he touched
her shoulder.

"Mitchell!" She sounded genuinely pleased. "How are you?"

They sat at a sidewalk cafe drinking coffee. Sunlight spilled
everywhere, drenching them, but he basked only in her presence. The undulations of the burlap sack cheered him; he was
soothed by its swish and ripple. He didn't mention his trou-
bles, only that he'd gone to South America and was taking
a break from cosmetic surgery. She said that an independent
label had offered The Gorgons a contract and they were preparing to record their first album.

"We are playing a show tonight. Perhaps you would
like to come?"

He smiled. That sounded like fun.

In a larger, cleaner club, The Gorgons' music erected
structures in the ether, hypnotizing the crowd. He stood at
attention toward the back of the room, unable to shift his
gaze away from the seething, churning sack. The night slid
away, they both drank too much, and he ended up back at
her place. Once she'd fallen asleep, her naked body prone
on the futon, he rose and walked down the hall to the
bathroom. He studied himself in the mirror, tried to recite
his mantra, but the words had fled his mind like a canary
whose cage has been torn open.

Before him, his features throbbed and shifted. Parts
were cut away, others enhanced. His face became the face
he'd glimpsed in the cracked mirror—the face he knew
was no illusion.

In the bedroom, he knelt beside her futon. As lightly as
he'd once scored flesh with a scalpel, he drew up the edge of
the burlap sack. Carefully, tugging first one side and then the
other, he worked the cloth up, sliding it in minute increments

out from under her cheek. The glowing red face of the clock beside the bed marked his progress—the removal of the sack took two hours.

When the last bit of burlap gave way, his heart ballooned. It roiled and rippled. On the other side of the window, the sun slathered its light across the sky. He felt like the boy who'd lost his mother in a department store, and his eyes sought the one thing that could bring him comfort. Viewed straight-on, the face was far more arresting than it had been in reflection, and as breaking day illuminated it clearly—entirely—he cried out. Cerulean eyes flew open, and pink lips, but he couldn't hear what they shouted. A droning, crackling sound deafened him. Sensation started to solidify. As she scrambled for the burlap sack, he watched the multitude of serpents twist and slither around her, and he understood how they felt—ecstatic, giddy, and free. Grinning, he gaped until he could breathe no longer, until pressure squeezed him from all sides, until the world hardened and was no more.

# NEVER, NEVER

*I* was fourteen when Mom married Captain Hook. My dad had vanished six years earlier, and I knew my mom was lonely, but I didn't think that gave her the right to wed the first one-handed swashbuckler who came down the pike. She'd started dating again when I was twelve, working her way through a commodities broker, a puppeteer, and an elementary school principal. Until the day she came home from work raving about the man she'd met while power walking at the docks on her lunch hour, however, I didn't really think I had anything to worry about.

"Some creep was following me, and out of nowhere this man swung in on a rope and landed between us." Mom acted out the scene in the middle of the kitchen. "He grabbed the creep by the throat with his left hand, and he shook his right hand, which isn't a hand at all but an iron hook, in the guy's face. He said if he didn't clear off, he'd eviscerate him. I'm sure Creep-o had no idea what 'eviscerate' means, but he ran for his life."

Her rescuer sounded like a badass, but I couldn't admit that to my mom. It had been just the two of us since I was eight, and though I no longer allowed her to cuddle me or tousle my hair, I secretly missed the closeness we'd once shared. I knew it wasn't easy—raising me alone, keeping us afloat on what she made at the bank—but the thought of her getting serious about someone drove me up the wall.

"He asked if he could buy me a cup of coffee, and I let him." She poked around in the refrigerator, pulling out leftover spaghetti and dumping the congealed, Tupperware-shaped blob into a Pam-coated frying pan. "We sat on a bench, studying cargo ships, listening to seabirds. He told me things about the ocean—what kinds of creatures live in coral reefs and how the moon's orbit controls the tides and what octopi do with their ink."

"How's he know so much about it?" I glanced up from the pair of battling, armored unicorns I sat sketching at the kitchen table. A kid who lived up the street had gotten me stoned after school, and when I'd started the drawing, I thought it would be really mind-blowing, but now that I wasn't so high anymore, I had my doubts. "Is he some kind of sailor?"

"He used to be." Mom piled spaghetti onto two plates and headed to the table with a green cylinder of parmesan cheese.

I plunged my fork into the mound of pasta and twirled. "What about now?"

"He just passed the Civil Service Exam. He starts at the Post Office next week."

Six years later, my stepdad would harass me to take the same Civil Service Exam, to get off my ass and do something with my life, to stop sponging off him and my mom— to grow up. "What's his name?" I asked.

"James Hook."

"Did he tell you what happened to his hand?"

My mom nodded. She used the edge of her fork to cut her spaghetti into bite-sized pieces, a habit that got under my skin. "It was eaten by a crocodile."

"No way! Was he trying to feed it?"

She shook her head. "The crocodile didn't bite off his hand. Someone cut it off and threw it to the crocodile."

"Jesus. Who cut his hand off?"

She gave me a sharp look. "A young boy. For years, James was consumed by thoughts of revenge, but he's recently realized what a waste of time and energy that was. He moved here to make a fresh start. He wants to live a normal life, and he's working through his feelings with a therapist."

I sensed that there was something she wasn't telling me.

"Peter," she said.

I looked up from my plate. "Yeah?"

"That's his name. The boy who cut off James's hand. His name is also Peter."

There turned out to be a lot my mom wasn't telling me about James Hook. For starters, he hadn't been a mere sailor but a ruthless pirate—the captain of a galleon called the *Jolly Roger*—and the crocodile who'd eaten his hand liked the taste of his flesh so much he now followed the man everywhere he went. True, the crocodile had also swallowed a clock that—in defiance of logic—continued ticking loudly inside him, but that didn't make the fact that he stalked us any less disturbing or embarrassing. The beast was always skulking in my mom's rose bushes or the pines that bordered our backyard. Every morning, he slithered off in pursuit of my stepdad's Toyota and hung around outside the Westside branch of the Post Office until closing time. Twenty minutes after my stepdad pulled into the garage, the crocodile would come ticking after.

Though he bore plenty of battle scars, Captain Hook was a good-looking guy, and he treated Mom like a queen. I can see now why she was so into him, but at fourteen I was mortified by my stepdad, and it wasn't just the crocodile. He was forced to wear the standard issue postal uniform during the week, but on days off he dressed in knee-length breeches, stockings, a red frock coat, and a wide-brimmed hat with a plume. His hair was even longer than mine, and it curled into black ringlets. My mom never seemed to notice the things that set her husband apart from other people—she saw only the man who'd rescued her from a lonely, loveless existence.

He tried to hide it, but every time he pronounced my name, my stepdad flinched. The Peter who'd cut off his hand was the leader of a gang of boys who'd ridden roughshod over Captain Hook and his crew back in Neverland, the place where he'd come from. I couldn't fathom how children got the better of grown pirates, and this became my favorite thing to rub in my stepdad's face. According to my mom, he was making great strides in therapy; little by little, he was letting go of his obsession with the other Peter. So I did my best to remind him just how disagreeable boys named Peter can be.

"Peter," he would say, his left cheek jumping, "after dinner, why don't ye help me with the dishes?" Once she married Captain Hook, Mom said goodbye to dishpan hands—he took over any household chore that involved splashing around in water. He would hang a lathered sponge from his hook and power through a sink full of greasy pots and pans in no time.

"Why should I?"

My mom's lips would part, but my stepdad would touch her arm with the tip of his hook—assuring her he had the situation in hand. "Because I asked ye to. We're family now, son, and it's high time ye started acting that way."

"You're not my dad."

"Aye. And I don't aim to take his place."

"Good, because you can't."

"I'm not attempting to."

"Well, you couldn't."

"Once again, that is not my intention."

Though I was no longer my mom's little boy, the ease with which Captain Hook had swept in and plundered her affection bothered me in a way I couldn't articulate. Brimming with teenaged indignation, I would leap to my feet and shout, "If my dad was here, he'd tell you where to shove that hook!" or "At least my dad never lost a duel to a ten-year-old!" or "Screw you, Captain Handless!"

I would slam my door and hurl myself across my bed. The ticking of the crocodile would drift through the open window, informing me that Captain Hook was nearby. I could picture him standing in the hall—staring at my bedroom door, touching it with the tip of his hook and the tip of a finger, longing to make things right with a boy named Peter, but not knowing how.

Before he met my mom, the closest my stepdad came to having family was Smee—his boatswain from the *Jolly Roger*— and when Captain Hook married Mom, Smee sat alone on the groom's side of the chapel. Short and round with wire-rimmed glasses, a bulbous nose, and flaming cheeks, Smee wore a stocking cap, and his accent was even thicker than the Captain's. Since Smee was my stepdad's closest friend, I wanted to dislike him, but that turned out to be impossible.

Smee carried with him at all times the finest weed I'd ever smoked. He said it came from an unnamed island in the Caribbean. He picked pounds of the stuff each time he went ashore, and I tried to explain to him that if he set up shop under the bleachers at my high school, he could make a killing, but Smee wasn't really profit-oriented. Since Captain Hook had given up pirating, Smee had found work on another ship; however, it was clear that my stepdad's retirement had been tough on him. During the reception, Smee and I locked ourselves in the bathroom, shoved a decorative hand towel beneath the door, and lit up one of the colossal joints I later learned were the only joints pirates smoked.

"Ye shoulda seen the Cap'n in the old days," Smee sighed. "He'd duel two men while steering the ship, eating a sandwich, and cutting his toenails. Never was there a braver nor a finer seafaring man."

"But he let a ten-year-old chop off his hand."

At the mention of the other Peter, Smee's blissful smile faltered. "That Peter's only a boy because he refuses to grow up. If he wasn't so tight with the Neverland Fairies, he'd be a man several times over."

Smee's lung capacity was astonishing; as he exhaled, smoke settled like pea soup fog over the counter, and I no longer saw a trace of myself in the three-way mirror. "Where is Neverland?" I asked.

Smee shook his head. "When it comes to Neverland, maps

are useless. Even if ye've been there, ye won't necessarily find yer way back. Most folks stumble on it by accident."

A metallic banging rattled the bathroom door, and my pulse quickened. "Smee? Is that ye in there?"

Smee cleared his throat. "Aye, Cap'n."

"I hope ye're not doing what I think ye're doing," my stepdad said. "Others need to use the restroom, ye know."

"Sorry," Smee said. "I'll be right out."

After a moment, my stepdad spoke again. "Smee?"

"Aye?"

"Young Peter's not in there with ye, is he?"

My eyes begged Smee to lie.

"Nay," Smee said.

"Good." I thought I heard retreating footsteps, but Captain Hook let out a sudden, menacing growl. "'Cause if he was in there doing what I *think* ye're doing, it would be the plank for the both of ye."

Whenever I got suspended or brought home a report card full of D's or stayed out past curfew on a school night—all of which happened more often as I scraped through high school—my stepdad threatened me with the plank. I didn't care about my education, however, and neither my mom's tears nor his threats swayed me.

"Peter!" Captain Hook shook my shoulder, waking me from a nap. It was a Friday evening early in my senior year. He still wore his postal uniform, and his black ringlets were pulled into a ponytail. He held my latest report card. "How are ye ever going to get into a good college with grades like these?"

"I don't want to go to college."

"What are ye going to do with yer life?"

I'd given this question some thought and was sure of only one thing—I couldn't imagine myself ever holding down some nine-to-five job just to make a mortgage payment every month. "I thought I might run away to sea."

My stepdad blinked rapidly. "Get up and meet me in the dining room."

At the table, Captain Hook sat bolt upright. I slouched across from him in a pair of cutoffs and no shirt.

"Ye've never even been on a boat," he said.

I shrugged. "So what?"

"Ye're serious."

"As a heart attack."

He nodded. "All right, then. Ye and I are going sailing. Pack a bag."

Though I wasn't thrilled at the prospect of being trapped on a boat with my stepdad, I looked forward to getting out on the open sea. Whenever Smee had shore leave, he thumbed his way to our front door, and while visiting, he slept in the top bunk in my room. He'd told me countless stories about the pirating life, and it seemed to me ideal—no cares, fresh air, riotous male camaraderie, adventure, infrequent bathing, constant weed-smoking. I was eager to get my sea legs and, after tossing a Rush tour shirt, a battered pair of underpants, and a toothbrush into a backpack, I strode into the kitchen and saluted my mom, who'd just gotten home from the bank.

"Do you guys have to do this tonight?" she said, kicking off her heels and opening the refrigerator. "I was going to make lasagna."

Normally I would have crawled across broken glass for a taste of her lasagna, but I couldn't pass up the opportunity to shed my landlubber status.

"Promise me you'll be careful." She gave me a tight smile.

"Relax, Mom." I bowed to kiss her cheek, which smelled of lilacs—a scent she'd worn for as long as I could remember. "I'll be with Captain Hook. What could go wrong?"

At the waterfront, my stepdad parked his Toyota and sat with his hook at rest on the steering wheel, his deep blue eyes fixed on the sun that drifted like a flaming balloon toward the ocean, igniting its surface. I was about to suggest we get moving when I noticed a couple of tears creeping down The Captain's scarred right cheek.

Climbing out of the car, we heard a clock ticking and spotted the crocodile slithering up behind us. He followed us down a dock, past dozens of small watercraft. Captain

Hook stopped beside a sport fishing boat with a high prow and an outboard motor, tossed our bags aboard, and—in the most graceful move I'd ever seen him make—leapt from the wooden slats of the dock onto the boat deck. He'd changed from his postal uniform into his usual weekend attire—frock coat, stockings, plumed hat—and stood for a moment, buckled shoes spread wide, arms akimbo, nostrils flaring.

"Whose boat is this?" I asked as he helped me clamber aboard.

"She belongs to Jerry." Jerry was one of his co-workers at the Post Office. Though he wasn't the quickest at the counter, my stepdad had proven his worth behind the scenes, and a month earlier he'd been promoted to Mail Supervisor. He could sort packages faster than a machine, using his hook to dig through string-tied parcels and fling them into their respective destination bins. He was also a master of paperwork, which the Post Office required in abundance—everything in duplicate and triplicate. Pink and yellow and white copies of invoices and work orders and reports hung handily from his hook.

"Why don't you have a boat?" I asked.

"Boats are expensive, Peter. Sit ye down."

I sat in one of the seats at the center console as he untied the mooring ropes. Stepping up to the controls, he ignited the engine and placed his hand lightly on top of the steering wheel. He depressed the throttle with the tip of his hook, and the vessel moved smoothly away from the dock. Once we'd cleared the other boats, he opened her up. We skimmed over the sea's mottled surface toward the sinking sun—a pinkish sliver on the horizon.

By the time he slowed the boat to a stop, the sun had vanished, and the star-pocked night spread like a domed blanket overhead. As swells tossed the boat, I became aware of how small the vessel was and how much smaller we were than the vessel. The silence was broken by a familiar ticking sound. Captain Hook shined a lantern across the water, and there was the crocodile—snout and yellow eyes peeking up from the salty sea. The beast swam around the boat in a diminishing circle. My stepdad led me toward the prow, where a thin platform protruded. The plank was designed for deep-sea anglers and guarded by a handrail, but beyond the rail the platform jutted several feet into empty space.

"After ye," Captain Hook said, and I stepped onto the platform. Fear and exhilaration shook me. I held tight to the rail. As I inched forward, I heard waves slap the hull below. The black surface of the sea threw back a wavering version of the firmament—winking stars, a tender crescent moon. When I reached the bend in the handrail, I turned and found my stepdad standing less than a foot from me. In the light of the lantern hung from his hook, his scarred face looked cadaverous.

"I guess ye know what time it is," he said.

I shook my head.

"I think ye do."

"Plank time?" My voice was weak.

"Aye."

The ticking grew louder, and I looked down. In the dark water, I could just make out the circling eyes of the crocodile. Captain Hook indicated that I should duck under the rail to the portion of the platform that dangled unguarded over the open sea. I shook my head. He removed the lantern from his hook and brandished the hook in my face. In the four years he'd been my stepdad, I'd never seen him threaten anyone with the hook. I dipped under the rail and straightened up on the other side, my whole body trembling.

Captain Hook lifted the lantern. He sighed. "I know where ye're headed, Peter, and I want to give ye the chance to change yer destiny. Ye remind me of meself, and it's not just the long hair, lack of respect for authority, and disregard for personal hygiene. All the years I was at sea, I thought I was happy. In a way, I suppose I was, but not in the way that matters."

His deep blue gaze pushed past me, into the darkened distance. A briny breeze blew my hair across my face, but I didn't dare loosen my grip on the rail. The swells beneath the boat grew larger. I was maddeningly aware of the circling, tick-tocking crocodile.

"Do ye know when everything changed? The day I turned forty. I woke up that morning, and everything kind of hit me. I didn't hate the other Peter so much because he cut off my hand—I was jealous of his ability to stay time. I thought about my crew, and I realized that even though we were aging, we were still living the lives we'd picked out as boys. I know at yer age this is hard to understand, but a man can only fill so many days with rum and sword-play and plunder. My life didn't *really* begin until I met yer ma, and knowing she waits for me at the end of each day makes the hook and the crocodile and the Post Office bearable. Given the choice between death and life without her, I'd walk the plank without hesitation."

I was an eighteen-year-old boy separated from a raven-ous crocodile by a thin strip of wood, and I'd like to say that in spite of this, I was moved by my stepdad's words. I'd like to say that his devotion to my mom touched me, that his attempt to steer me away from a life dedicated to depravity and vice was successful. But if I said that, I'd be lying.

"Peter," Captain Hook said. "Promise me ye won't run away to sea. Give college a chance."

Shivering with cold and fear, I promised; I crossed my heart and hoped to die. As the disappointed crocodile continued circling, my stepdad hauled me over the rail. I wanted to punch him in one of his deep blue eyes, to shatter his kneecap with a well-aimed kick, but I could only weep. As he hugged me tightly, a bitter concoction of humiliation and hatred seethed within me. Standing on the plank, I'd pissed myself, and I vowed that one day I would exact revenge on Captain Hook.

I *did* give college a chance, but I spent my time making rum -bottle gravity bongs and building a scale model of a Spanish galleon out of beer cans, so I failed out in my second semes-ter. I moved back to the split-level ranch Captain Hook and my mom had purchased after selling the bungalow where I grew up. For two years, I lost one crappy job after another: busboy, bagboy, delivery boy, pizza boy. My stepdad was con-

stantly after me to take the Civil Service Exam and join him
at the Post Office, and finally—fed up—I bought a stocking
cap, stuffed my belongings into a drawstring duffel, and did
what I'd threatened to do three years earlier.

Smee secured me a position with his ship, and on a blus-
tery spring morning, I strode aboard the *Starboard Suzy*, my
boots beating a satisfying tattoo on the weather-worn planks
of the deck. I dropped my duffel, inhaled the briny air, and
knew I was home. After six months at sea, you couldn't pick
me out of a grizzled, unshaven, foul-mouthed, stinking line-
up, one filled with men who from sunup to sundown wal-
lowed in their own filth, perversity, and carelessness. Even on
duty, we caroused, guzzling rum and smoking weed, and our
leisure was interrupted only by occasional, furious bursts of
looting, pillaging, and general badass behavior. There were
women—working girls in need of transport who bartered for
it with their flesh, and innocents we absconded with, many of
whom became enamored of one of our filthy band and had
to be disabused of their illusions. During my years aboard the
*Starboard Suzy*, I got involved with a couple of these girls,
but whenever the inevitable question came up, I refused to
turn my back on the sea.

I existed in the here and now, forgetting about life on land,
and each letter I received from Mom was a shock. She kept
me posted on what was happening back home—who'd gotten
married, who was pregnant, who'd died. My stepdad never
wrote. My mom insisted that since they'd made him Postmas-
ter he was just too busy, but I knew he couldn't forgive me
for embracing the life he'd turned his back on. Smee told stories about him to the younger crewmen, and with each telling,
Captain James Hook grew more mythic. In the beginning I
scoffed at these tales, but as the years passed, I started taking
strange comfort in the exploits of the young Captain Hook,
and I requested them of Smee more and more often.

"Peter. I've got to talk to ye, lad."

Technically I was no longer a lad the day Smee pulled
me aside and walked me toward the deserted aft deck. In
the twelve years that had passed since I'd climbed aboard

the *Starboard Suzy*, Smee had aged terribly. He weighed three hundred pounds and had lost most of his teeth. He was afflicted with a chronic, wet hack—one that could be heard in every corner of the galleon—and his sun-browned skin hung from him in flaps. He was no longer expected to loot or pillage—he'd become a sort-of ship's mascot. I was sure he was going to tell me he was retiring, and in truth I was relieved.

"I've a letter from yer stepda."

"Captain Hook?"

"Aye. He's sick, Peter. The doctors give him very little time. He hasn't yet told yer ma—he doesn't know how."

For the first time in years, I was forced to grip the rail for support.

"He didn't say it in so many words, but he needs ye, Peter."

At the thought of home—of my mom and stepdad and the mid-century furniture that filled their split-level ranch—a wave of nostalgia threatened to drown me.

"Peter?" Smee's eyes, cloudy with cataracts, searched my face. "Ye'll go, won't ye?"

"Aye," I sighed.

When I arrived, Captain Hook was barely clinging to life. I heard a ticking and spotted the crocodile slithering through the yard, forlorn. In the front hall, my mom embraced me for a long time, then pushed me toward the downstairs bedroom. The room smelled of infection and inevitability, and my stepdad lay on a hospital bed, eyes closed. He was attached to machines, some of which beeped, some of which pinged, some of which flashed lime green. He looked smaller than he had when I'd last seen him—on shore leave six years earlier—and his face was deeply lined. His black ringlets had been replaced by patchy gray stubble.

I stood in the doorway until my mom gave me another push. At my stepdad's bedside, I twisted my stocking cap nervously. His deep blue eyes fluttered open.

"Peter," he said, his voice no more than a whisper, "ye came."

His hand floated up—the nails overlong, the skin thin and papery—and I clasped it between my calloused palms.

"Ye're no longer a boy." He shook his head and his stubble scratched against the pillow. "I thought ye'd be a boy forever."

"You're thinking of the other Peter." I squeezed his hand. "The one who lives in Neverland."

"Nay." He shook his head again. "I know no other Peter."

A couple of years earlier I'd finally seen the boy who refused to grow up. Finding Neverland was as difficult as Smee had led me to believe when I was fourteen; in my years aboard the Starboard Suzy, we'd stumbled upon it only once. There, I'd seen not only the Fairies and the Redskins and the Lost Boys but also the other Peter. Whatever his actual age, he looked like a ten-year-old, and I was awed by the sight of him flying around on pixie dust. When he landed on the main deck of my ship, I showed him a picture taken at Sears not long after Mom married Captain Hook—a photo in which she and my stepdad and I wore matching sweaters. Peter's freckled features twisted with something like envy, and he went on at length about my mom—how pretty she was and how nice she no doubt smelled and how very lucky I was to have her—but he claimed to have no recollection of my stepdad. When I explained about Captain Hook's hand and the crocodile, Peter just shrugged.

"Sorry," he said, binding me to the mizzenmast as his Lost Boys carted booty out of our cargo hold. "I've known a lot of pirate captains. And I've chopped off a lot of hands. It's kind of my thing."

In the downstairs bedroom of the split-level ranch, a coughing fit seized Captain Hook, and his body convulsed, twisting this way and that. Once he'd quieted, I thought I could see right through him. As my long-awaited revenge for the plank-time incident, I'd planned to tell him the story of my encounter with the other Peter. I thought he should know that the boy who'd stolen his hand—the boy who'd haunted him, the boy whose name he hadn't been able to pronounce without flinching—had no idea who he was. Now, watching my stepdad examine his iron hook as though he was seeing it for the first time, my desire for revenge evaporated. He tugged on me feebly, and I bowed down 'til my ear hovered inches from his cracked lips.

"Ye smell like the briny deep." He pulled in a rattling breath. "Don't tell yer ma, but sometimes, I miss her still."

Captain James Hook was buried in a double plot he will one day share with my mom. As dirt mounded over his body, the crocodile who'd swallowed his hand years earlier—the creature who'd been biding his time, patiently awaiting a second taste—lowered himself to the ground and closed his yellow eyes. The clock ceased its ticking. The beast was dead.

The house filled up with mourners bearing covered dishes and condolences. People who'd worked with my stepdad at the Post Office came, as well as his regular patrons, couples he and my mom played bridge and took vacations with, guys from his YMCA basketball league, fellow Elks, and the woman who taught him to play the banjo. I didn't think any pirates other than Smee would show up, but a couple of crusty old marauders stumped around on peg legs, trying to blend in with the crowd.

"I can't believe Hook wasn't buried at sea," one of them growled, shaking his bald head. I'd had the same thought, but hearing it voiced upset me and I was tempted to defend my stepdad and his choices.

As night fell, I found myself standing alone in the backyard. I charted a course by the stars and imagined sailing away. Someone pulled up alongside me, and I knew without looking that it was Mom.

"I'm surprised you guys never took a cruise," I said. "Or bought a boat."

"I would have been happy to do either, but James never wanted to."

"He loved you more than life."

"I know." She squeezed my arm. "Guess you'll need to get back to your ship soon."

I tried to picture the Starboard Suzy's stout hull cleaving deep waters, but I saw only the other Peter standing on her main deck, studying the portrait of my family—his small face etched with envy. "Thought I'd stick around," I said. "Find an apartment. Look for a straight job."

"Are you sure?"

I wasn't, but I stooped and kissed her cheek. It still smelled of lilacs.

"Wonderful," she said. "I'll go put on some coffee."

I was used to constant motion—to adjusting my frame to the undulations of the sea—and I was having a hard time balancing on solid ground. I wondered how long it had taken my stepdad to adapt. I imagined Captain Hook in his plumed hat and frock coat, holding a spyglass and sextant, standing in the backyard after my mom had gone to bed, charting courses by the stars, checking the direction of the wind, picturing it filling his sails. Maybe he'd never really turned his back on the sea. Maybe he'd tolerated life on land by fantasizing about open water. Maybe it was this that had enabled him to walk the plank into the chasm of manhood—the plank that stretched before me now, the board upon whose surface my hesitant feet had just been set.

# DEDICATION

*I* dedicate this, the eleventh edition of a text written in my obstreperous youth, to a man with whom I enjoy a unique symbiosis. Without whom I would not be the individual I am today. A man who is a slave to numbingly cold logic. Whose powers of deduction are transcendent. You know who you are, my dear S—H—, and you know why I dedicate this printing to you. When *The Dynamics of an Asteroid* was first published, it proved to be beyond the abilities of any living critic; to this day the book remains indecipherable even to the world's leading mathematical minds. Though not all its mysteries are as enticing as "how did Moriarty survive the fall from the Reichenbach," the text contains many riddles—puzzles at which I thought you might like to try your hand. Perhaps this volume will keep you company during the interminable nights on which—fueled by a seven-percent solution of cocaine—you will do nothing but think of me, and wonder.

—Professor James Moriarty
London, March 15, 1893

# DYNAMICS

The book you're reading is called *The Dynamics of an Asteroid*. Its germ was implanted, like a seed that houses a *Sequoiadendron giganteum* in its entirety, into my cerebral cortex when I was nine years old. On the day he announced his intent to leave Mother for his research assistant Akbar—a placid, dusky youth of whom I was quite fond—Father presented me with a text entitled *A Treatise on the Binomial Theorem*. Its contents burst like Lilliputian rockets into my frontal lobes, the area of the brain concerned with planning, decision-making, goal-setting, and relating the present to the future through purposeful behavior. Over time, original notions and ingested data would coalesce around this germ like the accreting layers of nacre that form a pearl, and the thing would blossom. But when I was nine—on the day I last caught sight of Father—I read only three pages of the text he'd given me before collapsing on the polished floor of his study. It seemed that I grasped mathematics in an *a priori* fashion, and as Mother applied cold compresses to my cheeks, I dreamt of my arithmetical future.

I did not, dear reader, allow the frailty of my sex to stand in my way, though I must admit, bringing my dream to fruition has not been easy. But once Father traipsed with Akbar off to exotic locales like Patagonia and Tanzania and Albuquerque, Mother became overly indulgent.

Father still supported us in the manner to which we were accustomed, and I eschewed the frocks and slippers and tea sets and beaded handbags and parasols under which Mother attempted to bury me, insisting instead that she purchase the latest mathematical journals and treatises. If she refused, I would throw myself down in the foul, cobbled streets, smashing my fists until I drew blood. I was that rarest of children—an infantile insomniac—and I spent my sleepless nights poring over texts, including my rumpled, dog-eared copy of *A Treatise on the Binomial Theorem*, a book penned by Professor James Moriarty when he was just twenty-one years old.

Because I was Father's daughter, I was given dispensation to study mathematics at Durham University, where the same Professor Moriarty chaired the department. Though I yearned to dress in trousers and a waistcoat, to paint on a mustache and blend in with my classmates, Mother insisted on arraying me in the latest Parisian fashions, and I bobbed among my fellows like a brightly plumed, beribboned, whalebone-corseted seabird. In classes they spoke not a word to me; I felt only their withering, sidelong glances. In spite of my natural aptitude—in spite of my love of all things algebraic and geometrical—to them I was no more than a punchline. But I wasn't bothered. I concerned myself only with Professor Moriarty.

And he concerned himself with me, though he was quite skilled at concealing his interest. From the moment our eyes met, I understood that our destinies were inextricably entwined. Of course we couldn't let on, so in class, he would not call on me—even when I was the only student with a hand raised. He was not slighting me, nor was he offended by the notion of a female mathematician; he was obliged to ignore me. So as not to make the others jealous. So as not to be accused of favoritism. Whenever I visited his office and found the door barred but heard his movements on the other side, I did not allow this to upset me. It was the way things had to be. Our relationship was so very clandestine that we ourselves never discussed it.

When I arrived at Durham, Professor Moriarty had chaired the department for seven years. Thin, unsmiling, and introspective, he had the sort of high, domed forehead that speaks of profound acumen. He was unmarried and known for his infrequent but spectacularly destructive alcoholic binges. Among the faculty, his reputation was one of difficulty and coldness. He was thought by many to be cruel. But none could deny his brilliance, and his theoretical work was respected by all. He was at work on a new text, one that—it was said—would make *A Treatise on the Binomial Theorem* look as if it had been penned by an untutored child. Speculations that the book would ascend to previously unattainable heights of pure mathematics flew around the department, enticing me, whetting my appetite, stoking my flames. Professor Moriarty rarely drew his curtains, and from the box hedge outside his neat stone cottage, I sighted him night after night—sitting in his shirtsleeves, collar unbuttoned, scribbling in a fevered lather. With the aid of powerful Belgian Porro prism binoculars—a gift from Father and Akbar, who'd finally stopped globe-trotting and settled in Antwerp—I was able to spy the text's title page. *The Dynamics of an Asteroid.* When I read the words, I collapsed on the dusty ground in a fit identical to the collapse I'd suffered in Father's study nine years earlier, only this time, Mother wasn't there to apply compresses. Once I was able to stand, I saw that I'd split my taffeta dress. Holding the fabric together over my frilly underthings, I made my way back to my well-appointed rooms, where in a fit of unrivaled astronomical inspiration I began writing this book.

The pages I tucked into Professor Moriarty's desk drawers and slipped into his overcoat pockets prompted him to approach me at last. "How do you know about this?" he would say. "Are you spying on me?"

He would upbraid me, threaten to report me, but I knew he would never give me away. Professor Moriarty was frightened of his feelings. He was unnerved by the turbulent gulf of emotion upon whose edge we both teetered. He wasn't equipped to deal with what was happening between us. He was a theoretician—comfortable only with suppositions, things fleeting and ephemeral. He had no idea how to contend with a flesh-and-blood relationship like ours, so I forgave him. I always forgave him.

"This is my book," he would say. "You can't write my book."

"But it's not," I would respond. "It's not the same book at all."

And it wasn't. My *Dynamics of an Asteroid* was less a text of pure mathematical theory than an arithmetical story of love. Professor Moriarty's and my love. It cast us in the roles of celestial bodies, and it explicated—in an algorithmic, measurable fashion—the details of our attraction, of the galactic motions that had drawn us together. It was a celebration of romance, albeit in mathematical terms. What can I say? I may be a theoretician, but I am not entirely immune to the stereotypical tendencies of my sex.

"I won't allow my work to be usurped," Professor Moriarty said, stepping forward until his chest was inches from mine, "by an unbalanced female." We stood in his garden, where he'd discovered me at the awkward hour of six o'clock in the morning crouched behind a blue hydrangea. Weak, milky light crept over the landscape, and a vaporous mist stood in the atmosphere. My mind barreled down branching neurological pathways, overcome by the proximity of Professor Moriarty. His breath hit me in the face, echoing my own—the stale respiration of the insomniac—and the pupils of his dark eyes vanished in the morning gloom.

"Please," I said, placing a hand on his forearm. I wanted to tell him that my book was not simulacrum but tribute. Homage. That it had been burgeoning ever since *A Treatise on the Binomial Theorem* burst into my frontal lobes when I was nine years old. "Let me help you."

His lips said no, but his eyes said yes, and *The Dynamics of an Asteroid* became a collaborative effort. He never again remarked on the pages I slid into his battered brown satchel or left folded in his postbox. In class he continued to overlook me, but at night, peeking through the windows of his cottage with my Porro prism binoculars, I spied him consulting my work. Once he'd transformed them, I hardly recognized my own notions, but they pushed his text to mathematical heights that made me dizzy and weak in the knees.

As the academic year drew to a close, I received a letter penned in Akbar's neat, slanted script. It seemed that Father had passed away; apoplexy had struck as he sat at his desk in the dead of night, straining to work out a brand-new formula. *I know he failed you,* the tender-hearted Akbar wrote, *but I would be remiss if I did not tell you how much he loved you. How often he spoke of you and with what pride. He was a brilliant but difficult man, and I think I am a better person for having loved him. I am sending the manuscript of his last book which, with his dying breath, he bade me give you.*

I'd never been able to blame Father for leaving Mother, but I'd always been miffed by his abandonment of me. He was the person who'd shown me the power of measurable computation, however, the person who'd set my feet on a path strewn with postulates and logarithms, and though I hadn't seen him since I was nine, the news of his demise undid me. I was blindsided by despair. When I opened the box that contained his manuscript, my vision blurred, but I read the title through a veil of tears.

*The Dynamics of an Asteroid.*

*Dearest,* read the accompanying note, *I sent a copy of this to your mentor Moriarty a year ago but never heard back. It is missing something—something I've become too aged and enfeebled to ascertain. Read it for me and expound on the theories I have put forth. Say you'll collaborate with your father on this—his final text.*

I longed to crack the pages, to scrutinize every term and numeral, every computation, but I didn't dare. If I shunned Father's manuscript, I wouldn't be faced with undeniable similarities. I wouldn't be forced to reevaluate my position on the man around whom I planned to build my life. My illusions would remain unshattered, my foundations unshaken. I secreted the manuscript under a loose floor-board in my closet. I continued working with Professor Moriarty on his *Dynamics of an Asteroid*. I tried to wipe my father's text from memory; it remained, however, lodged beneath the surface of my consciousness like a nagging, infinitesimal shard of glass.

We are none of us originals, I told myself, those of us who theorize and suppose. We read. We borrow. There is no helping the cross-pollination of ideas. Though they matter to us, though they set our minds racing and our feet on certain paths, in the grand scheme, texts mean nothing. Within their rigid covers one finds only a plethora of pages—thin, flimsy, easily torn. The assertions put forth do not exist unless one speaks the language in which they are written. What a thing to have built my life around, I thought as I sat long into the night, pulling volume after volume from the shelves in my rooms, poring over them until the phrases and numbers blurred together into one long, meaningless verse.

Once *The Dynamics of an Asteroid* was published, Professor Moriarty's mystique mounted. He did not give me credit for my collaboration, but I forgave him. I always forgave him. When I took my doctorate, I accepted a teaching appointment at Durham in order to remain close to him, but our love continued to be a theoretical affair. In time innuendo began to gather around Professor Moriarty. Whispers of his involvement in gambling, racketeering, extortion. Of a plot to rid himself of several rival mathematicians speaking at a conference in one fell swoop. Finally—under a cloud of suspicion—he was forced to resign his chair and move to London.

From then on, Professor Moriarty was said to employ his superior intellect in the role of criminal mastermind. Just last year, word came that he'd plunged from a waterfall in the Swiss Alps while grappling with a sleuth of great renown. This seems to me as unlikely, however, as the purported exploits of said sleuth—who is rumored to have written a monograph on the myriad varieties of pipe and cigar ash, and to be able to pronounce whether or not a man has done murder based solely on the condition of the suspect's boots. These conceits strike me as the work of a fiction writer—a not-very-inventive one at that.

I like to think, instead, that Professor Moriarty is holed up in a basement room, shunning sleep, diligently working on a new text. Pausing mid-sentence to gaze through the barred window at the hurrying calves of passersby, he dreams of me. He wonders if I am in good health. He considers what the twenty years that have passed since last we saw one another might have done to my face. My body. He hopes I understand how much I meant to him. That I understand why he had to leave.

I *do* understand. It's all right there in his *Dynamics of an Asteroid*. If one knows where to look. If one peers between the formulas and beyond the theorems and beneath the postulates, one can decipher a stirring arithmetical tale of duty, sacrifice, and undying devotion. It's no shock that critics cannot fathom the book—who can squeeze mathematical meaning out of a love story?

Texts are by nature variable. Editions come and go. One mistake in the ordering of typeface gives an entire print run new meaning. Each of us writes our own *Dynamics of an Asteroid*, and one version is quite interchangeable with another. When I finally opened Father's manuscript, voluminous tears streaked my face. There, represented numerically, was his undying love for Akbar; I even thought I detected a hint of his love for me. As I now sit writing my own *Dynamics*, the version that once blossomed like a *Sequoiadendrum giganteum* hovers still in my mind. I can recall the algorithmic love story I abandoned in order to assist Professor Moriarty with his rendition. But the book I now write—the book you now read—is a pastiche. A potpourri. I'm accustomed to collaboration, and I've attempted to embrace all the disparate *Dynamics* that have come before. And those that will come after.

# THE TRAGEDIE OF CLAUDIUS, PRINCE OF DENMARK

Witness this army, of such mass and charge,
Led by a delicate and tender prince;
Whose spirit, with divine ambition puff'd,
Makes mouths at the invisible event;
Exposing what is mortal and unsure
To all that fortune, death, and danger dare,
Even for an egg-shell.

—*Hamlet*, Act IV: Scene 4 s

## Act I

They made the pact six weeks after the sickness descended on the King. One day he was their sagacious, silver-tongued father—warring with lusty Norwegians, guzzling mead, dandling chambermaids on his armored knee—the next, he was a man entirely obsessed with poultry. Chickens. Ducks. Pheasants. Geese. A plentiful supply of fowl was always on hand at Elsinore, but the King ordered his aides to scour the countryside and purchase every available bird. Colossal coops were constructed beneath the windows of his private solar, and he could be found in one of these fetid, wood-and-wire structures each morning before first light—wrapped in bedclothes or nothing at all—tugging warm, newly laid hen fruit from beneath feathered backsides. Once his basket brimmed, he would enter the closet of his young sons—crowing to wake them. Placing an egg in each boy's palm, he would demand to know what pulsed beneath its shell.

The first time neither Claudius nor his brother Hamlet knew how to answer, and their father flew into a rage. "Life!" he shrieked, seizing the shoulders of first one boy and then the other, rattling them until their heads lolled brokenly, until their eggs smashed against the floor, painting broad streaks of yellow over the flagstones. The next morning, once they'd assured him they felt the life force quivering within each hen fruit, the King told his sons the eggs contained the reborn souls of those whose lives he'd stolen. Not only those he'd slain with his own hands, but those to whom death had traveled outwardly from his person, like concentric ripples on the surface of a pond. Infantrymen and mercenaries. Nobles and craftsmen. Women and blameless babes.

"If I keep them safe and warm," he said, "they will hatch. I will beg their forgiveness and raise them to relive their purloined lives!" The King nestled hundreds of eggs beneath fur-lined blankets, into the eiderdown with which he'd covered his mattress. For three weeks he perched atop this nest, leaving only to collect more hen fruit from the coops each morning, covering sheets of parchment front and back with infinitesimal script, straining to discern the soft crackle of shell.

Claudius and Hamlet were sleeping when the eggs started hatching, when their father burst into their solar, dragging the Queen by one unsullied white hand. "They are coming!" he cried as his family scuttled through the dim halls of Elsinore. "The souls of the Departed!" The King's torch shed uncertain light on elaborate, floor-to-ceiling tapestries depicting familial forebears on the field of battle, tromping over a bloody carpet of fallen foes. Weaponry flashed on the walls. Spears. Maces. Battle-axes. After mounting the stairs and passing beneath dozens of buttressed archways, they entered the King's solar, where the monarch dropped to his knees. His mattress had been stripped of blankets, and the eiderdown that covered it was littered with eggshell fragments varying in hue from pure white to speckled brown. The rank chamber was awash in the strident cheeping of hungry newborn fowl.

"Please," the King said, his hands folded, his eyes shut. "You must forgive me. All of you must forgive me."

The Queen stood in the doorframe, both hands pressed to her mouth. With a muffled cry, she sank to the rush-covered flagstones as Hamlet strode forward to stand beside the King. His brother was only a year his senior, but Claudius couldn't picture himself ever catching up to Hamlet, whose demeanor was that of a man despite his spindly limbs, despite his cowlick and hairless cheeks.

"My lord," said Hamlet, "there are no Departed. Open your eyes. They are chicks and ducklings and goslings."

The King hadn't shaved or dressed or bathed or cleaned his teeth in three weeks, and he bowed his wild, wooly head over the eiderdown. Stroking his beard, he studied the hatchlings—membranous lids stretched over black eyes; vulnerable throats; beaks wide open; damp, bedraggled feathers.

Claudius moved forward. He touched his father's naked shoulder. "They are hungry, my lord," he said, his tears splashing his bare feet. "They want to be fed."

The King rose. He crossed to the door, stepped over his prone, sobbing wife.

"Where are you going?" said Hamlet.

Their father paused—filling the doorframe like a broad, grizzled, naked specter. "I must feed them," he said. "It is the only way they will ever forgive me!"

So Elsinore was transformed into an elaborate, drafty, absurdly well-fortified fowl coop. "Grow quickly, my sons," said the Queen as she pecked Hamlet and then Claudius on the cheek and made ready to depart the castle for the distant home of her cousins. "My husband has no male relatives, and Denmark sorely needs you." The King conscripted the princes, and alongside an army of porters, they hand-fed hundreds of hatchlings as more eggs were laid and carted inside to incubate. Hamlet and Claudius were charged with wrangling the adolescent birds that soon overran the castle—clucking, squawking, roving in gangs through the lofty halls, insinuating themselves into cabinets and pantries, distressing the cooks and the maids and the Lord Chamberlain, bathing in colossal bowls of spiced wine, napping in the Chamber of State, defecating on the throne of Denmark. The King had eggs nestled into eiderdown atop the princes' beds, and when they weren't busy with extant birds, Hamlet and Claudius were expected to sit like broody hens upon these nests.

"Fortinbras of Norway is amassing his armies," said Claudius three weeks after their mother's departure, "and the King won't consider abandoning the Departed to oppose him."

Hamlet slid off his nest and stalked to the window. "Your eggs, Brother," said Claudius, but Hamlet spat on the floor.

"We are Denmark's only hope," Hamlet said, gazing across viridian fields that swept from Elsinore to the frothy gray sea. "The time has come to act."

Beneath his backside, Claudius felt a small shifting.

"He is no longer fit to turn back the fierce Norwegians." Hamlet approached Claudius's bed. "We must take care of the King."

Claudius's palms went damp, and his heart knocked around in his chest. Beneath him, stifled cheeps and taps sounded.

"If we do not," Hamlet said, "there will be no more Denmark."

"What if his condition is temporary?" said Claudius. "What if he regains his senses in a month, or a week?"

The brothers thought of the King as they'd last seen him—bowing naked before a gang of quacking drakes and honking ganders in the Chamber of State, weeping and begging the birds' forgiveness.

"We cannot afford to wait," said Hamlet.

Hamlet would rule—of that there was no question. Though he was but thirteen, he comported himself like a man. Unless something untoward happened to his brother,

Claudius would never be King of Denmark. He expected
to feel some prick of envy but felt only relief. The knowledge that he would not be ultimately responsible for the
lives of so many Danes comforted him; still, he was greatly saddened by his father's fate. In a decrepit alchemy text
in Elsinore's library, Hamlet had discovered a purportedly
painless poison—one concocted from black mushrooms
that grew in the vicinity of the castle. The brothers would
pour this potion into the King's ear canal as he slept.

"Come down from there," said Hamlet.

"But my eggs."

"Damn your eggs! Get down here!"

Claudius slid off his nest and stood face to face with
his brother. Hamlet thrust out his left hand, palm-up, and
indicated that Claudius should do the same. He produced a
dagger, pressed the tip to his own palm, and sliced open his
flesh. Claudius fought to hold his arm steady as his brother
did the same to him. Once blood flowed from both boys,
Hamlet gripped Claudius's left hand with his own. He used
a yellow scarf—one their mother had left behind—to bind
them tightly together. "We must now make a pact," he said,
"one that can never be broken."

Red seeped through the scarf, and Claudius felt faint.
He heard cheeping as if from a great distance.

"If ever one of us shows signs of the sickness that has
ruined our sire," Hamlet said, "the other must take care of
him as we will now take care of the King."

Until that moment, Claudius hadn't realized his brother
feared anything. He wondered what else Hamlet was hiding.

"Say you swear it, Claudius."

"I swear it."

"And we take the secret of his death to our graves.
Swear it."

"I swear."

After Hamlet departed in search of the dusky mushrooms they required, Claudius snatched the blankets from
his mattress and found a multitude of hatchlings in the
eiderdown. Some had pierced holes in their shells, others

were half-out, struggling with all their might to be free.
Only one bird had shed his casing completely—a damp
gosling with black eyes. Wobbling on new legs, he advanced
on Claudius, who inhaled sharply, for in that moment, the
gosling seemed possessed—driven—as though he were
animated by the spirit of a man rather than a beast, as
though his ebony eyes were full of mad accusations.

"Forgive me," Claudius whispered. "You must forgive me."

Claudius never told Hamlet about the accusatory gosling,
but in the days that followed, more and more of the birds
overrunning Elsinore seemed to him to exhibit human char-
acteristics. Glancing into a crowd of chicks or a gang of geese,
he would catch flashes of featherless, flesh-toned skin. Once,
he thought he spied a tiny, malformed hand. A week after the
princes made their pact, as they dined on roast mutton,
porridge, and smoked herring, their father galloped into the
dining hall, clutching a rooster under one arm and a pheasant under the other. He announced that the Departed had
started forgiving him. He danced around the walnut table,
crooning to the birds. Hamlet fixed Claudius with a weighty
look, and Claudius tried not to weep. The time had come.

In the dead of night, the brothers managed to avoid
treading on a slumbering bird as they crept across the
King's solar—which bore the distinct air of a barnyard.
They found their father curled on his right side, ensconced
in fowl, a smile on his hirsute face. He clutched to his chest
the thick sheaf of parchment that for weeks he'd been covering with cramped script. Claudius's heart pumped wildly,
unevenly—he feared it would wake the King. The brothers
had agreed that they should each administer half the poison, but Claudius's hand trembled, nearly spilling the inky
liquid. Once the flagon was empty—once the deed was
done—Hamlet plucked the parchment from his father's
lifeless grip. The brothers returned to their solar, where
Hamlet studied the King's scribblings.

"Names!" he said, letting the sheets spill over the flagstones. "Meaningless names."

Claudius gathered the pages. He attempted to straighten and arrange them. "The Departed," he said and started weeping. His father had crossed only two names off the list.

Hamlet knelt before Claudius. He lifted his brother's chin. "Hush," he said. "Would the King of Denmark have wished to live that way?"

Claudius did not feel qualified to answer.

"Had he been in possession of his mind, he would have begged for death," said Hamlet.

Claudius knew his brother truly believed this, and jealousy pulsed through him. He longed for such conviction.

"Now we turn to Denmark—to protecting her from ruthless Norway," Hamlet said. A gaggle of goslings waddled out from under Claudius's bed, and Hamlet rose. He aimed a sharp kick at the birds, and as they scattered, one slammed into the stone wall—permanently silenced. "And we rid ourselves of this damned poultry!"

The day Hamlet was crowned King, he banned all fowl from Elsinore. Birds infesting the castle were routed from their hiding spots, rounded up, and slaughtered. Eggs tucked into eiderdown-covered beds were collected and shattered. The coops outside the old King's solar were torn down and, along with egg remnants and feathered corpses, burned in a conflagration on the castle grounds. The Queen returned to Elsinore and stood between her sons, watching flames lick the leaden sky, a perfume-soaked scarf masking her face. "They smell beastly!" she cried. "Though not as bad as when still they lived!"

At her husband's funeral she wept politely, but Claudius wanted his mother to break down, to howl and launch herself onto his father's boxed remains. It was assumed that the King had slid away in his sleep, and in preparation for burial, he'd been bathed, shaved, and dressed in battle armor. Clutching his gold-handled broadsword, he looked like the King whom Claudius had grown up with—the man who'd ceased to exist once his strange convictions about reincarnation and poultry overtook his life. During the ceremony, Claudius was struck by the urge to conceal a couple

of duck eggs in his father's coffin—reborn souls to accompany the Danish King into the afterlife. Somehow, Claudius
had grown fond of the clatter and the stench and the drifting feathers. He'd grown accustomed to caring for chicks
and goslings—to their pulsing, daily affirmation of life—
and Elsinore now seemed to him unbearably silent and ster-
ile. He thought about smuggling a couple of hen fruit into
the castle, hiding them from his brother, incubating them in
his bed. But he feared spying a glimpse of his late father in
one of the hatchlings.

## Act II

"It is not murder to put a mad animal out of his misery,"
King Hamlet said to Queen Gertrude, whose wolfhound he
had that morning eviscerated with his saber. "It is kindness."

"Radolf was not mad!" Gertrude hammered her husband's chest with her fists. "I could have calmed him!"

Hamlet caught her wrists. "He would have torn you
apart along with the child," he said. "How then would I have
carried on?"

"You can take my brother's word, madam," said Prince
Claudius, entering the Great Hall. "The hound was deranged.
I swear it."

"I do not care who swears it." Gertrude wrenched free
of Hamlet, swaying on her feet. Her jaw might have been
cut from the quarry west of Elsinore, and she advanced
on Claudius until her distended stomach knocked into his
groin. "I will never believe it."

She'd been hand-picked by Claudius's widowed mother,
who'd returned with the willowy, ginger-haired girl from
a summer visit to her cousins two years earlier, on King
Hamlet's twenty-fifth birthday. Claudius was roaming the
grounds when Gertrude approached Elsinore on a dappled
gray mare, her hair aflame in the sun. He understood her
function instantly—she was an incubator, acquired for the
germination of his brother's seed. If Claudius thought of

her as a commodity—a broodmare—it was almost possible to ignore the ache that throbbed through him whenever he caught sight of her. For more than a year, he scrupulously avoided the new Queen of Denmark, but on a stormy night in the stables of Elsinore, everything changed.

Fourteen years had passed since the castle was overrun by reborn souls masquerading as poultry, but that experience had kindled in Claudius a persistent fascination with gestation and birth. His brother's ban on fowl still stood; whenever a cow calved, a sheep lambed, or a dog whelped, however, Claudius was present. His knowledge of animal nativity rivaled that of the stable master, and he enjoyed attending at difficult births—thrusting his soaped arms into the birth canal of a mare, checking for dilation of her cervix, looping a rope around her fetus, guiding it toward life. During such a birth nine months earlier, as Claudius eased a foal from the dark interior of its mother, he'd wondered—as he always wondered—if he would recognize in the emerging newborn a Norwegian he'd cut down in battle, or be confronted with the grizzled face of his own father. If he would finally get to ask the question his brother the King had never had trouble answering. *Did we do the right thing? Would you have wanted to live with your madness?* But the foal that appeared was just a foal. His mother was too weak to tear the membrane that wrapped him, so Claudius did it for her. When the newborn suckled at last, when Claudius stood to stretch his aching body, Queen Gertrude stepped from the shadows of the stables and pressed herself against him.

Claudius's skin was painted with blood, his hair pasted to his head with sweat, but Gertrude did not seem to care. She stroked his chest, and he wound his arms around her. Previously, Claudius had made love to chambermaids and shepherdesses by rote; Gertrude seemed a brand-new order of being, however, one to whom the rules did not apply, and he endeavored to explore every part of her. As she clung to him, her legs encircling his waist, he concentrated on burning every sensation into memory. Rough stable beam pressing into his back. Moonlight glancing off the hollow between her shoulder blades. Wide eyes of the foal, examining them with newborn wonder. As thunder cracked, shaking the night, Claudius envisioned the path of his seed—exiting his testes, rushing down the shaft of his penis, bridging the gap between them, swimming into her uterus, fertilizing a waiting ovum. Afterward, he curled his body around Gertrude, trying to memorize her with his fingertips. Eventually she sat up, pulled on her nightdress, and fled the stables. Neither of them had spoken a word.

"My lord," Gertrude said now, extending a hand to Claudius in the Great Hall, her swollen stomach dangling between them. "Will you see me to my solar?"

As they walked the wide corridors of Elsinore, Claudius studied dust motes drifting through shafts of light, concentrating on the pressure of her hand in his. He wanted to fall down before her, to tear open her gown and affix his lips to her brimming belly. No matter where he went, he felt the life force flowing from Gertrude, seeping into every corner of the castle. Six weeks had passed between that night in the stables and the King's announcement of her pregnancy to his assembled aides and courtiers, and Claudius had spent nine months worrying about the creature that would emerge from her womb. Would he know the difference between son and nephew? Would Hamlet? Would the child be one of the Departed, reborn at last? Would he emerge with the shaggy face of the old King?

"How now, my lord?" Gertrude said as they mounted the stairs.

"Well, madam."

"Can *you* explain why your brother murdered my wolfhound?"

Despite what Claudius had said in the Great Hall, the animal was never mad, and he wouldn't have thought Hamlet capable of such strange cruelty had he not seen it with his own eyes. Radolf had been a proud beast—a wedding gift from Gertrude's parents. She'd nursed the pup by hand, and he'd slept nightly at the foot of her bed. Each morning at dawn, the hound had accompanied Hamlet and Claudius as they toured the castle grounds, discussing affairs of state. That particular morning, as they wandered through a copse of flowering ash trees, the King drew his saber and rounded on Radolf. The wolfhound threw himself down on a yellow carpet of leaves, rolling over to expose his pink, hairless underside. Claudius's stomach turned as Hamlet plunged his blade into the animal just north of his testes and sliced upward, opening the hound to his ribcage. Radolf whimpered piteously, his eyes full of confusion and pain. He paddled the air for a moment before expiring. Claudius gaped at his brother, who stood breathing heavily, watching red runoff pool on yellow leaves.

"How now, Hamlet?" Claudius had finally managed to say.

The King knelt to wipe his blade clean on Radolf's fur before sheathing it. "Death to all enemies of Denmark," said he.

The scene had troubled Claudius deeply, but he could not betray his brother. Though he'd taken the reins as a mere boy, Hamlet had driven off Fortinbras of Norway and markedly expanded Denmark's borders. Under his rule, Denmark had enjoyed twelve years of accord and abundance, but the weight of leadership had taken its toll on the King, and the brooding aspect of Hamlet's nature had come to the forefront during his reign. Claudius did not envy his brother; at times the Prince was plagued by the guilty knowledge that he'd never shouldered his share of the burdens of state.

"A sickness of mind took Radolf," Claudius said now to Gertrude. "Just as King Hamlet stated."

They drew near her solar, and the Queen slowed their pace. "But my lord," said she, dropping her voice, "have you failed to notice the sickness of mind that seems to be taking the King?"

Claudius knew his brother was prone to black moods, but it turned out that Gertrude had seen the King carrying on agitated, one-sided conversations. She'd found him on his knees, railing against—or pleading with—an apparent specter. Once, in the night, he'd kicked open the door of her closet, waking her from slumber. "Do you think it possible," he'd asked, sweat beading on his forehead, his fingers digging into the soft flesh of her arms, "for the dead to stalk the living?"

Claudius's left hand twitched. He lifted it, studying the scar that traversed his palm—the indelible mark of a fourteen-year-old pact. "Speak to me no more," he said to the Queen. "These words like daggers enter in mine ears." The hot scent of blood seemed to rise out of empty air, and Claudius felt faint. Gertrude took his hand, splaying it flat against her abdomen, and he felt the force of life brewing within her. It coursed up his arm—traveling like a lightning strike through his body, reviving him.

"My lord," said the Queen, "what think *you* of ruling Denmark?"

Claudius's mother had started knitting woolen items as soon as she learned of the embryonic heir's existence. In nine months she'd filled her closet with brightly colored wrappings for the child who would, any day, spring forth from the prison of Gertrude's flesh. There was hardly room to move in the Queen Mother's solar and not a surface left uncovered, yet she kept on, her pewter needles flashing in an unnatural frenzy. As soon as she finished a blanket or hat or stocking, she tossed it atop a teetering pile and started another. She hardly left her closet, hardly ate, hardly slept. Each time Claudius saw her, he was certain she'd shrunk. The fetal Danish heir seemed to be driving her, and in so doing, siphoning her life.

"How now, madam?"

The Queen Mother looked up from her flying needles to proffer her son a white cheek, and Claudius wondered how she remained so lovely. At her feet sat Lord Polonius, his hands wrapped in yellow wool, prattling on about sailor's knots and thicknesses of shoe leather and whether wigs made of horse or human hair are more attractive and durable. Before Polonius could launch into another soliloquy,

Claudius shooed him from the room. The small man bustled out, huffing, after bowing to kiss the Queen Mother's hand.

"Polonius's wife is heavy with child, yet he spends his days closeted in your solar," Claudius said. "Has the impending birth of an heir forced my brother to rebuff you at last?"

His mother's needles ceased their clacking. "I don't know what you mean, my lord."

Her appetite for younger men had been an open secret even before the death of the old King. She'd never cuckolded her husband, however; an understanding had existed between them, and before he gave up the pleasures of the flesh for the company of fowl, the old King had exercised his reign over the courtesans and chambermaids of Elsinore with astounding frequency and stamina. Claudius didn't know how much time passed between his father's death and the beginning of his mother's unnatural relationship with his brother; he only knew that one morning three years after Hamlet was crowned, he'd encountered the King emerging from her closet at dawn, hair disheveled, boots in hand. "How goes it with the Queen?" Claudius asked, but he'd gotten no response. Instead, his brother glued his eyes to the flagstones and slunk away.

Claudius tried to envision some other explanation, but castle gossip soon confirmed his suspicions, and for months, the company of the incestuous pair tied his stomach in agonizing knots. He and Hamlet had sworn never to speak of their father's death, but when he'd been drinking, Claudius was tempted to break into his brother's solar, to demand to know if they'd killed the old King for his own good and for Denmark, or so Hamlet could have unfettered access to their mother. One night Claudius woke to find his brother's silhouette perched on the edge of his mattress. "There was nothing between us while the Old King lived," Hamlet said. "That you must believe."

Claudius never knew if he'd dreamed this visit, but he found that it did not matter. Real or imagined, Hamlet's assurance lifted a weight from him. Nine years later, when

Gertrude arrived on her dappled mare, Claudius wondered whether matrimony would put an end to the relationship, but rumor had it that the players simply learned to be more discreet.

"Polonius keeps my affairs in order," his mother said now, resuming the rapid rhythm of her knitting. "King Hamlet would be well advised to take advantage of his services."

Claudius and Hamlet had known Polonius—the son of their mother's favorite waiting lady—since they were boys. Claudius felt sorry for the awkward, verbose young man, but Hamlet had never been able to abide him. As King he steadfastly refused to allow Polonius to wait on him at court.

"He is most knowledgeable," the Queen Mother continued, "and could advise the King on a great many subjects. Shipbuilding and animal husbandry and commerce . . ."

"What does Polonius know of madness?"

Her needles fell silent.

"You are close to my brother the King," Claudius said. "Perhaps closer than anyone. Does Hamlet ever put you in mind of the man our father became at the end of his days?"

The hands that had come to embody unstoppable motion— the fingers that for months had been driven by an invisible engine—froze. The Queen Mother stood. The unfinished stocking slid from her lap, and her needles clattered to the flagstones. "What are you asking, my lord?"

"Have you noticed anything unnatural about King Hamlet?"

As she stepped forward, Claudius noticed a lilac vein pulsing in her throat. He thought for a moment that she might strike him, but instead she fell against him with a sob. Once she'd quieted, she said Gertrude's wolfhound wasn't the only innocent creature his brother had executed of late. The Queen Mother had recently happened upon a ghastly scene on the grounds of Elsinore. As she crested a hill, she noted mounds of red-streaked white dotting the lower field. Drawing near, she discovered ewes—dozens of them—each with twin lambs beside her. Every animal's belly was slit, its throat cut. The fleecy bodies were still warm. Pooling blood steamed in the cool morning. The Queen Mother discovered a weeping shepherd boy curled behind a nearby haystack.

"The King, my lady," he said in response to her query. "King Hamlet murdered my flock."

The night before the birth of Prince Hamlet—son of King Hamlet and heir apparent to the Danish crown—Claudius dreamed a river of blood. Its source was the moist opening between the thighs of Queen Gertrude, who, thick with the life of her offspring, had grown to monstrous proportions. She no longer resembled the girl who'd ridden toward the castle with hair aflame or the woman whose body Claudius had once explored in a damp, dark stable or even the swollen mother-to-be who'd taken to grunting and cursing as she hoisted her burden up and down the castle stairs. She resembled nothing so much as a whelping wolf, and Claudius knew if he got too close, she would tear out his throat.

The old King was there, not dressed in armor and carrying a broadsword but as Claudius had last seen him awake and alive—wrapped in dirty bedclothes, hair flying, a rooster tucked under one arm and a pheasant under the other. At the sight of him, joy rattled Claudius. He tried to embrace his father, but the old King darted away. Claudius chased him, splashing through the river—which was calf-deep and rising, flowing through Elsinore. "Life!" the old King shrieked. "Life!" His father dove into the red stream, and Claudius waded after. He plunged his arms in, searching for Gertrude's child—for the origin of the life force that crackled in the close air of the castle. The river now reached his chest, but Claudius was a strong swimmer, and he struck out, fighting the current, paddling upstream. King Hamlet appeared on the bank. "Remember our pact, Brother," he said, extending his left hand. With a howl, Gertrude birthed a colossal white egg, and Claudius threw his arms around the bobbing hen fruit. He heard a tapping and felt the shell shift, but suddenly he was too exhausted to hang on. He saw that his brother and Gertrude had been washed into the river, and he knew the child would drown with the rest of them. Claudius woke to find his pillow soaked with tears and someone—somewhere—screaming as though they were being torn apart.

The screams belonged to Gertrude, who'd gone into labor at dawn. Claudius found Hamlet standing outside her solar, fingers plugging his ears. "My wife could wake the Departed," said the King. Over the protestations of her ladies, Claudius pushed into her closet. He rubbed her back, hips, and thighs as though she were a foaling mare. Gertrude grasped his arm with enough force to snap bone, and she kept up her wailing nonstop—a piercing sound that drove all from the castle who were not involved in the birth. The child still hadn't appeared at nightfall, but Claudius didn't begin to worry until Gertrude's screams ceased. Shortly before the sun rose, her glistening, ashen face flopped against her cushions, and he knew she'd reached the end of her strength. He spit on his fingers and inserted them into her vagina. Bypassing her dilated cervix, he touched a foot—the babe was breech. Claudius tore the scarf from the Queen's head and worked it inside her. He looped it around the child's ankles and tugged until he felt a shift. Then the boy was in his hands.

The limp Danish heir was an alarming shade of blue. Claudius cleared the muck from his mouth and covered it with his own. The slight chest rose and fell a dozen times before Claudius heard a cough followed by a thin scream. He wrapped the infant in a blanket and tucked him beside Gertrude, who could scarcely lift her head. "His father," she said. "Give him to King Hamlet." His brother had entered the room at the sound of the cry and stood studying the babe with wide, uneasy eyes. Claudius thought he might crush the boy or snap his neck or swing him by his feet, smashing him headfirst into the wall, but instead, Hamlet did something Claudius had never before seen him do. He wept. As his brother's tears baptized the future King, Claudius felt the life force ebbing from the room. Exhaustion settled over him. The last thing he saw was the rush-covered floor flying up to greet him.

## Act III

Not since fowl freely roamed the corridors had there been such activity at Elsinore. Along with Polonius's children—Laertes and Ophelia—Prince Hamlet engendered more mayhem than a gang of adolescent ganders. When they weren't playing conquest or assassin, when they weren't forcing the king's fool Yorick, like a pack animal, to cart them around, when they weren't sliding down staircases on serving trays or swinging through the sylvan grounds on vines made of torn bedclothes or tipping over sleeping cows, the children would wallow naked in mud puddles, then creep indoors to lie in wait behind a tapestry or rack of gleaming sabers. At the sight of a laden chambermaid, they would leap out, keening wildly, waving filthy arms, shaking mud-caked locks. Releasing whatever she held—a tray of roasted meats, a bowl of mulled wine, a brimming chamber pot—their victim would scream and flee to the pantry to tell the harrowing tale of the ogres she'd encountered outside the Great Hall. And once, when Prince Hamlet and his accomplices decided a Norwegian spy had taken up residence at Elsinore, they rounded up every maid, scullion, porter, and cook and herded them into the kitchens, where they bound them hand and foot. After conducting grueling interrogations, the children lost interest in their game and vanished. Their suspects weren't found until hours later, when the Queen Mother happened into the kitchens to find out what would be served at supper.

"He's so like his father at that age," the Queen Mother often said as Prince Hamlet grew, but Claudius could not see it. This prince seemed to him the very embodiment of childhood—a phase of life his older brother had bypassed entirely. As a boy, King Hamlet had engaged in play only when forced.

"How does young Hamlet put you in mind of the King?" Claudius asked his mother. "My brother was such a grave child."

"My lord," said she, "memory is mainly a matter of perspective."

Claudius did not know it, but this was the last conversation he would have with his mother, who'd withered since the birth of Prince Hamlet ten years earlier. Each day she seemed to lose mass, and her face—which had remained plump and unlined well into her fifth decade of life—began folding in upon itself. She took to wearing a veil and rarely left her solar, choosing instead to spend hours on her knees in prayer, a posture in which Claudius was unaccustomed to seeing her. She even spurned the company of Lord Polonius, who hovered outside her closed door—pacing and rhapsodizing about the significance of human contact.

The Queen Mother hadn't left her closet in weeks when, one misty morning, she ventured out at dawn. She'd been confined to the ground floor for five years, but she made her gradual way up the staircase, pausing periodically to wipe her face with a tattered yellow scarf. Up she went—up and up—past Prince Hamlet's closet, past the solar she'd shared with her late husband. She wound round a newel staircase, climbing the tower in the west curtain wall. Shoving open the immense door that led to the battlements took all her strength. A formidable wind gusted over the wall walk, and the Queen Mother braced herself. She glided along the notched parapet, past crenels and merlons, a tiny veiled figure, eyes probing the clotted mist. When a voice spoke her name, she froze. She'd come in search of him, but she now wished she'd never left the safety of her closet. That she'd instead lain upon her cot to expire in peace. Sinking to the damp stones, she closed her eyes and folded her hands beneath her chin. Too late, the Queen Mother had grasped the advantage of madness, and it was for this that she'd been feverishly praying.

"Take me," said she. "Please soften death's blow."

When a cold hand brushed her cheek, she tried to cry out, but she could manage no more than a whimper.

That afternoon two shepherds discovered her body at the base of Elsinore's west curtain wall. Her veil had flown off as she plummeted, but a yellow scarf—one streaked faintly with red—remained clutched in her hand. The shepherds would argue for hours—for years—over whether the Queen Mother's expression was one of fear or rapture.

The day his mother was buried, King Hamlet had been seven years absent from Elsinore. Three years after the birth of the Danish heir, Norway had once again threatened Denmark, and the King gathered his forces and rode off to war, leaving Claudius behind to act as Steward of his home and nation.

"When Fortinbras last moved against us, I fought beside you," Claudius protested after his brother informed him of this decision, "and I recall the warm blood of countless Norwegians running between my fingers. Why are you now leaving me to cower in the keep with women and children?"

"Brother," King Hamlet said, kneading Claudius's shoulder, "I cannot risk both our lives. Prince Hamlet is but a babe, and should I be struck down in battle I will depart this world eased by the knowledge that Elsinore and Denmark are safely in your hands."

Kings Hamlet and Fortinbras pushed one another back and forth across contested lands, and though Claudius kept the soldiers of the garrison in a state of readiness—drilling them daily—the fighting never came near Elsinore's isolated coast. This was a great relief to Claudius, who despite his protestations had no desire to fight. The heat, the stench of rotting flesh, the screams of the injured and dying, the panic and sleeplessness that had beset him constantly during the campaigns he fought as a boy of thirteen and fourteen—these were etched indelibly into his cognizance, and he could not face them again. He thought that he'd managed to conceal his pusillanimity, but obviously his brother had discerned it.

"The Danish heir needs you, my lord," Queen Gertrude said to Claudius three years after King Hamlet's departure. "You must now start playing the part of father as well as uncle."

As they walked the halls of Elsinore, the childish shrieks of Prince Hamlet and Polonius's children rang off the stone walls. "In which role do you think I will be more convincing?" asked Claudius.

"We have no idea when King Hamlet will return, if he returns at all," said Gertrude. "And what a boy needs foremost is a father."

But in his dealings with young Hamlet, Claudius never managed to approximate paternal authority. Gertrude begged him to discipline the prince, who was as wily and silver-tongued as the old King had been in his youth. Claudius, however, was in awe of the boy. He enjoyed watching him race through corridors and over verdant fields, terrorizing staff and livestock, filling Elsinore with his kinetic energy. Filling it with life. When Claudius wasn't drilling the guards or attending to affairs of state with Polonius—who under pressure from his mother he'd named Lord Chamberlain—he shadowed Prince Hamlet in his play with the fool Yorick, or steadfast Laertes and gentle Ophelia. Claudius saw something burning inside young Hamlet, and he was at once drawn to and frightened of the flames.

The day after his mother's funeral, Claudius sat in a dim corner of the Great Hall and watched the prince— wrapped in bedclothes, capering around the room. The boy approached Polonius's children, who lay curled side by side on the rush-strewn floor. He stretched out atop them, rubbing his hands together and giggling. Soon his playmates started quivering. They made tapping and cracking noises. Cheeping sounds. Young Hamlet slid off the children as they pushed up to their knees and opened their mouths, flapping their arms against their sides. He tore hunks from a loaf of bread, masticated them, and spit them into the mouths of his playmates. Once he'd fed them, Prince Hamlet fell down in front of Laertes and Ophelia, who continued cheeping and fluttering their hands.

"Forgive me," the boy said. "You must forgive me."

Most of Elsinore's residents knew nothing of the sickness that had taken Claudius's father. King Hamlet had pronounced the topic *forbudt* when he declared the ban on fowl twenty-four years earlier, and Claudius could count on one hand the remaining chambermaids who'd been at Elsinore during the old King's reign. One was senile, one was mute, and the other was no fool. With his brother gone seven years and his mother now dead, Claudius had started to think he was the only person alive who recalled the final days of the old King. Had it not been for the sheaf of yellowed parchment—now locked in a chest in Claudius's solar—on which his father had catalogued the names of the Departed, he might have thought that the fowl coops and the eiderdown nests and the hatchlings never existed in the tangible world. That they had been illusions. Figments of his fancy. When Claudius saw Prince Hamlet and his playmates acting out their pantomime, tears blurred his vision, and he wanted to take the children in his arms. He wanted to shake them. He wanted to place warm hen fruit in their palms and shout, "Life!" In trying to determine who at Elsinore could have mentioned the old King's obsession with poultry to Prince Hamlet, Claudius came up with only one possibility.

"Certainly not!" Polonius sputtered when Claudius approached him in the Chamber of State.

"You might not have spoken inadvertently?" said Claudius. "In front of Laertes or Ophelia?"

"My Lord Claudius!" the Lord Chamberlain said, glancing over his shoulder in spite of the fact that they were alone. "I have not spoken of the old King in better than twenty years! To do such a thing would go against a multitude of my most treasured and deeply held beliefs. My honor. My code of ethics. My dedication and strict adherence to not only the spirit of the law but its letter—its flawless immutability."

And though Polonius was a colossal windbag, Claudius felt the Lord Chamberlain was telling the truth. *How then*, he thought later that afternoon as he weighed one of Gertrude's breasts in his palm, *is it possible for Prince Hamlet to know of the old King's sickness?*

"What has my brother told you of our father?" Claudius asked the Queen, whose skin glimmered with perspiration, whose head rested on his stomach, whose red hair cascaded in waves over his genitals. They'd held out for years, but the death of the Queen Mother had undone them both. After his conversation with Polonius, Claudius had discovered Gertrude alone in her solar, weeping. As they shared reminiscences of the woman they'd buried only the day before, exchanging comforting words and soothing caresses, their bodies underwent an urgent transformation. Claudius and Gertrude found themselves replaying the scene that had taken place eleven years earlier after a difficult foaling in the stables of Elsinore.

"King Hamlet never spoke of him," said Gertrude, whose bare form was fuller but, to Claudius, more comely than when last he'd seen it. "I asked your mother once, and she said her late husband was a benevolent monarch, a skilled commander, and a liberal lover. She said they'd grown apart as they aged, and that only long after his death—only as she entered her dotage—did she realize how much he'd meant to her. How much she'd loved him."

His mother had never spoken to *him* of her feelings for the old King, and Claudius felt a stab of envy. He gathered Gertrude to him and kissed her fingers, her elbows, her shoulders. He probed the divot in her clavicle with his tongue. She grasped his penis, which, since the day he'd first seen her riding toward Elsinore, had always stiffened at the merest thought of her. "We must use caution," said she. "Should King Hamlet return from war with Fortinbras, a child will not be easy to explain."

But once the gates had opened, there was no stemming the flood. Claudius and the Queen coupled whenever the mood took them. As the first rays of the sun touched the pillow on which their heads rested. Up against a flowering ash or in a pile of dying leaves. For the first time, Claudius wondered if love was not, in fact, a ruse created to goad mankind into procreation. When Gertrude sighed and said, "Would that you had been crowned in place of King Hamlet," Claudius imagined that he might have made a good King. But when Prince Hamlet asked for tales of his father, Claudius enumerated the exploits of the Danish King—daring raids he'd led, stout enemy soldiers he'd battered to death with his bare fists—and was forced to recall his own cowardice and inadequacy. Queen Gertrude acted on Claudius like a drug—their relationship was a waking dream from which he had no desire to be released. He longed to imprison her in his solar, to wallow with her, to shun the company of others, and he began to wonder if the old King had felt the same way about his poultry.

One evening Claudius caught sight of Prince Hamlet roaming the corridors wrapped in bedclothes, and he followed the boy at a distance. Up the prince climbed, up the central staircase, up the newel stairs to the tower in the west curtain wall. Claudius shadowed him over the battlements as the sun sank—flaming red on the horizon. The boy's bedclothes glowed in the gathering gloom. When the prince came to an abrupt halt, Claudius concealed himself behind a piece of the parapet. The boy spoke, but Claudius heard no answering voice. Peeking over the wall, he saw the Danish heir standing upon the walk—unquestionably alone. The prince's mouth was in motion. He grinned and gestured as though deep in conversation with the air.

What game was young Hamlet playing? What had brought the boy to this part of Elsinore—to the very place where the Queen Mother had drawn her last breath? Claudius had spent more time with his mother during her final months than ever before, and the proud woman, who'd never been forthcoming with the details of her life, had battered him unceasingly with tales of her girlhood. Tales of the early days of her marriage. Tales of a Denmark that no longer existed. Her mind had grown muddied, and she tended to weave disparate storylines into bizarre amalgams. Into the narrative of a reception held for a Swedish official, she would insert an anecdote about the old nanny who'd raised her. While describing the handmade lace veil she'd worn to be wed, she would shift suddenly into the story of her younger brother, who'd bled to death after being gouged by a wild boar. Claudius was riveted by her revelations until the day she placed a shuddering hand upon his knee and started conversing quite candidly about her relations with men.

Her litany of lovers was as confused as her narratives; she jumped around in time from early experiences with stable hands on her father's estate to her affair with Lord Polonius. She named several men with whom she'd lain while married to the old King, and though it was difficult to make sense of her chronology, one in particular seemed to have become her lover during the year that separated the births of King Hamlet and Claudius. In speaking of this courtier, now long deceased, she nodded and patted Claudius's knee.

"He's the one, my lord," said she. "I believe he's the one."

Claudius had been careful not to dwell on the implications, but now, crouched in the fog ushered in by nightfall—a dense haze that cloaked the battlements of Elsinore—he could not stop himself. Was he only half-brother to Hamlet? Did no blood tie him to the old King? Had he not committed patricide after all? The stones of the parapet pressed into his back, and Claudius imagined the veiled figure of the Queen Mother winding around the wall walk. Why had she left the safety of her solar? What had driven his mother to mount the summit of Elsinore?

A glowing white shape emerged from the fog. It drifted toward Claudius, and his heart throbbed. His stomach hollowed. Hairs rose on the back of his neck. As the specter drew near, Claudius stood to meet it, but at that moment he realized he was looking at young Hamlet wrapped in his bedclothes.

"I have something for you, my lord," the boy said, extending his fist. He didn't seem surprised to find Claudius crouched on the battlements, spying. Claudius opened his palm, and the prince dropped into it a smooth ovoid object. One that glowed with a faint blueness. The egg was far smaller than the hen fruit Claudius had tended as a youth—the egg of a starling, perhaps, or another migratory bird. He closed his fingers around it. He thought he might burst.

"The old King bade me give it you," said Prince Hamlet. "He says it is one of the Departed."

◆ ◆ ◆

Despite Claudius's best efforts at incubation, the blue egg would not hatch. Eventually he wrapped it in a cloth and locked it away in the chest alongside his father's list of the Departed. When he pressed Prince Hamlet for details about his encounter with the old King, the boy said he'd met the ghost by accident. He'd been unable to sleep one night and had wandered up to the battlements in search of cool breezes. The reckless prince hoisted himself onto the curtain wall and raced around it, scrambling onto the merlons and leaping down into the crenels. At a point, he realized he was being trailed by an old man with wild gray hair. An old man wrapped in bedclothes. An old man clutching a rooster under one arm and a pheasant under the other. Young Hamlet had never seen such birds. He doubled back to ask about them, and when he drew near, he saw that the man was less than substantial. Parts of him seemed to wink and shimmer and fade.

"My son is your father," the old man said. "In life, I was King of Denmark."

He told Prince Hamlet that his birds had once been animated by the souls of people long dead. That they kept him company in the afterlife. "The Departed want only one thing," he said. "To be reborn. We hate death. We hate to see it extinguish life. If ever a specter asks you to kill—beware." Since that night, the prince had ventured up to the battlements to visit the spectral old man many times, and he'd learned about the history of Denmark, and also about the life cycle of poultry. As young Hamlet spoke of his grandfather's ghost, Claudius lay on the floor of Elsinore's library, feeling as though his bones had dissolved. He told himself the boy had always had an overactive imagination, yet the Danish heir knew things he could not possibly know.

"Has he spoken to you of his death?" asked Claudius.

"He said he slid away in his sleep."

Was this proof that Prince Hamlet was inventing a story? Or had the old King—curled up with his fowl in peaceful slumber—never known that his own sons took his life?

"Did he mention the Queen Mother?"

Young Hamlet nodded. "He asked me to tell her he was roaming the battlements."

"When?"

"Two weeks ago."

So this had prompted his mother's climb to Elsinore's zenith. Had she hoped for a last-minute reconciliation with her husband's ghost?

"Has he said anything of me or your father?"

The boy nodded again. "He said you search for the Departed but cannot see them. And your brother sends too many to the afterlife. Those he has slaughtered are angry with the Danish King."

The next day Claudius started haunting the battlements. He spent his nights roaming the wall walk. He gave up food and sleep. He abandoned Gertrude's bed. He descended into the castle only to attend to essential state business. "How now, my lord?" the Queen said repeatedly, her gentle voice infused with hurt. "Have I done something to displease you?" Claudius was forced to turn his head and flee, lest her spell weaken his resolve. He staked out the spot where he'd seen young Hamlet talking to empty air. He rubbed his eyes and squinted into the ether. He raced over top of the curtain wall—scrambling onto the merlons and leaping down into the crenels. He called the old King's name. He howled and shrieked it. "Am I not who I have always believed?" he cried. "Am I not your son? How does one measure the madness of a King? Answer me! Show yourself! Please!" Even when he grew weak with hunger, even when the sun's heat made him swoon and shudder, Claudius saw nothing out of the ordinary. He saw only stones and mortar and mist and sky and the viridian grounds of Elsinore, and the vast gray sea that stretched out to her east.

When the young prince ventured up to the wall walk, the boy claimed that he could no longer see the old King. "You have driven him away, my lord," said Prince Hamlet. Claudius seized the boy's shoulders. He shook the Danish heir until his dark head lolled brokenly from his neck. When the rage that had descended on him lifted, Claudius tried to apologize—to embrace the boy—but after skewering him with a venom-infused look, Prince Hamlet fled.

Claudius did not understand how the souls of the Departed could be so close and yet so far. Whenever he fell into uneasy sleep on the rough stones of the battlements, he dreamt of Prince Hamlet slaying him with a sword and a cup. He died begging the boy's forgiveness every time.

## Act IV

King Hamlet annihilated Norway, slaying Fortinbras in close combat and annexing vast tracts of land before returning to Elsinore. When he dismounted and strode toward Prince Claudius, Queen Gertrude, and Prince Hamlet—who stood together before the castle's vaulted entryway—Claudius recoiled. Evidence of the King's bloody work was etched into his face. He looked too old to be the man who'd ridden to war twelve years earlier, and he stooped as though saddled with a great, invisible weight. He embraced Claudius and Gertrude, but when he turned to fifteen-year-old Hamlet, the boy ducked behind his mother. "Don't you know me?" said the King, and his voice had changed. It was full of grit and gravel, and Claudius wondered if this Hamlet could be an impostor. "I am your father. I am King Hamlet." But the prince—whose boyhood playfulness had been usurped by petulance, who now spent hours on end locked alone in his solar, whom Claudius had recently come upon peering through the keyhole into Queen Gertrude's closet, watching her bathe—did not respond.

"Forgive him, my lord," said the Queen, pushing the boy's dark hair out of his eyes. "The prince was but a babe when last you met."

Gertrude had not prepared her son for King Hamlet's return as—in truth—she'd never expected it. It wasn't until she received word that her husband had triumphed over King Fortinbras and was on his way home to Elsinore that full understanding crashed down upon her. The Danish King had not perished in battle. In her mind he'd long slumbered beneath the rimed earth of a Norwegian fjord, as spectral as Radolf—her dead wolfhound. When he shed his armor and clambered on top of her that first night, he seemed to Gertrude a worm-eaten corpse enveloped in the miasma of the tomb. She wanted to break free of his putrid embrace and run shrieking through the corridors of Elsinore, to seek refuge in the arms of the man who'd spent twelve years playing the part of husband and father. Love for Claudius had long stalked Gertrude—hovering just out of sight, crouching in the nooks and corners of the castle—and once it arrested her, she gave herself over to it entirely. She convinced herself that Claudius had sired her son, but as young Hamlet grew and—in looks as well as temper—started mirroring her absent husband, Gertrude had to struggle mightily to maintain her illusions.

"Why cannot you get along with Lord Claudius?" she asked the boy two weeks before King Hamlet's return. Gertrude perched on the mattress in the prince's solar. Young Hamlet sat on the floor, his twisted, tear-stained face in her lap, his fingers clutching her skirts. "He wants only what's best for you."

"Lord Claudius is not my father," the prince said.

"He is your father's brother as well as Steward of his home and nation. And he has cared for you since you were a babe. You don't even remember the King of Denmark."

"I could say the same of you, madam."

"Oh, Hamlet," Gertrude sighed, "you cleave my heart in twain."

Perhaps it was guilt over their illicit love, but neither she nor Claudius had ever been able to censure the prince. Instead they'd allowed him to run wild, and much as Gertrude hated to admit it, her son had become a willful and spoiled young man. In him, she searched for signs of the tenderness she'd first marked in Claudius in the stables of Elsinore sixteen years earlier but saw none. The first time she'd stumbled upon Prince Hamlet making love to Polonius's daughter Ophelia—who'd blossomed into a maid of matchless beauty—Gertrude was seized by the vague, jealous stirrings of a mother who discovers her only son's interest in another woman, and she secreted herself behind a wall tapestry in the Great Hall to observe their interaction.

"Fair Ophelia!" Prince Hamlet had cried, dropping to his knees before the girl, burying his face in her abdomen, grasping her slight waist. "What gift will you have of me?"

"It matters not," said Ophelia, her fingers smoothing his dark hair. "Your words, my lord, composed of such sweet breath, always enrich your tokens."

"What then shall I compare thee to? What bloom? What nimble creature?"

"I know not."

"A nymph," Prince Hamlet said, rising and taking the girl in his arms. "An immortal sprite that haunts a weeping brook, drifting in eternal, blossoming beauty."

As Gertrude watched the prince cover Ophelia's mouth with his own, as she watched the defenseless maid collapse against him, her heart thumped—not with anticipation—but with dread. Ophelia was nothing like her bombastic father. Her good spirits and grace enlivened the gloomy haze that often settled over Elsinore, and Gertrude had always been fond of her. At times she imagined the girl was her own daughter. The thought of a union between Ophelia and her son would have pleased Gertrude if she hadn't become thoroughly convinced, at the moment she discovered the budding romance, that Hamlet's intentions were less than honorable. That he was an arrant knave and not to be trusted.

"It's time the Danish heir saw the world that exists beyond the castle grounds," Gertrude told her husband a few days after his return to Elsinore. "His worldview is narrow, and he lacks training and discipline. Fine schools abound in Brussels and Paris, in Zurich and Wittenberg."

"What think you of this notion?" King Hamlet asked Claudius as they roamed the grounds at dawn—just as they'd done years earlier with Gertrude's wolfhound. "Of sending the prince to school in Wittenberg?"

"It will be good for the boy," said Claudius. "He has much growing up to do."

Though he'd tried his best, he'd never managed to win over young Hamlet, whose resentment seemed to mount with each passing day. Claudius had dragged the prince to the stables of Elsinore on numerous occasions—conscripting his services in a difficult calving or foaling—but the boy was never inspired by the experience. "Cannot you feel it?" Claudius would ask as they sat afterward, half undressed, streaked with blood, watching a newborn suckle. "The force of life?" But the prince would merely shrug. Spit on the floor. His maturing face echoed the visage of King Hamlet and was just as inscrutable. As he became a youth, the prince grew increasingly hostile toward Claudius, and their disagreements escalated into altercations. Claudius thought the boy provoked him intentionally, and a fury such as he'd never known began to seize him in the midst of these arguments. He wanted to grab the sneering youth and shake him as he'd once done on the battlements of Elsinore, but he wanted to do more. To bruise and bloody the impudent boy. To put him in touch with agony. Such unbidden, violent thoughts distressed Claudius, and a few days before King Hamlet's return, he attempted to engage the prince in conversation about the only secret they'd ever shared. But young Hamlet claimed to have no knowledge of the ghost that once roamed the battlements of Elsinore.

"I'm sorry, my lord," said the boy. "I know nothing of the old King."

Claudius now slowed his pace to match that of his brother, whose war wounds had left him with not only a twisted back but also a marked limp. Claudius's increasingly brutal thoughts weren't prompted only by young Hamlet; violent acts occurred to Claudius as he sealed state documents, as he dried the flanks of a newborn foal, as he lay coiled in a naked knot with Gertrude. His brother spoke of gutting and beheading Norwegians, of snapping spines with his bare hands, and Claudius wondered if savagery were inherited. A disease swimming in the blood, transmitted from one generation to the next. If his muddled mother had gotten her chronology mixed. If the old King had sired Claudius after all. Had his own brutal leanings merely been more deeply buried than those of his brother? Or had Claudius and Hamlet sealed their fate with the unthinkable act they'd committed as boys? Had they been cursed from the moment they tipped the flagon over the ear of the old King?

"Death to all enemies of Denmark," said King Hamlet.

In the hazy morning light, Claudius faced his brother—whose eyes glinted, whose lips were flecked with spittle. Hamlet shuddered, his gnarled hands tearing at empty air, before collapsing in Claudius's arms. This was the second time Claudius had seen his brother weep, and as he knelt in dew-glazed grass, rocking Hamlet and stroking his crooked back, a strange sense of superiority bloomed in Claudius. The Danish King had been reduced, drained of that which had always characterized him—the semblance of strength and conviction. Claudius felt, in that moment, stronger and more certain than ever before.

"When I rode off to face Fortinbras, I was sure I would never see Elsinore again," said Hamlet. "Sure that if I threw myself into every skirmish, I could not survive repeated clashes with the Norwegians. During the battles you and I fought as youths, I grew accustomed to killing and maiming—to the heat of war—and in truth, I found the years of serenity that followed difficult. Nothing ever satisfied me like soldiering, and having left behind an heir and you, Brother, to care for Denmark in my stead, I was prepared to accept a soldier's ultimate fate.

"My lust for blood overtook me, and I became a true berserker. Exterminating without cease, without heed. As the years stretched on, and I kept killing but did not die, I began waking nightly from miasmic dreams, my heart galloping out of my chest. I used to fear nothing so much as madness, but during these twelve years, I made a discovery. The more lives a man steals, the more cause he has to fear death. Now that I am a broken heap—now that I should be making my peace with this world—I cannot imagine leaving it. I cling to life with every ounce of strength I possess, for I am terrified of what awaits me after."

The sun burned the haze from the grounds of Elsinore. Claudius and Hamlet knelt in the grass, gazing at one another without speaking. Each thought of the old King as last they'd seen him alive—ensconced in fowl; clutching a sheaf of parchment to his chest; a grin on his grizzled, slumbering face.

Polonius stalked the corridors of Elsinore with murder in his heart. Before his father had been killed in one of the old King's many Norwegian campaigns, he'd told Polonius that by discerning the prevailing winds, by culling the favor of those in power, one could get ahead from the most humble beginnings. It was toward this that Polonius had tirelessly worked all his life, and now—when he'd finally achieved some semblance of status—it was all to be snatched away.

As a boy he'd been terrified of the clucking, roving gangs of geese and drakes that roamed Elsinore, and when the Queen Mother took him and his mother along to the home of her cousins, he'd been heartily relieved. But once they'd returned, Polonius had followed King Hamlet's directive—never speaking a word about the old King's madness. He'd done everything he could to cultivate the favor of the Danish King and Lord Claudius, comforting the aging Queen Mother, upon whom he'd doted as a boy, sharing with her intimacies he should have reserved exclusively for his lady wife. Thanks to the generosity of Lord Claudius, Polonius had spent twelve years serving as Lord Chamberlain of Elsinore—a post for which he was the ideal choice. A master of efficiency and organization, Polonius was nothing if not modest and retiring. And always willing to yield to those with more knowledge.

Now that was all over. Lord Claudius had been apologetic, but there was no changing his brother's mind. When they were boys, Hamlet once painted Polonius with honey and bound him to an anthill. He'd pushed him out of trees, breaking one of his arms. The King had never been anything but a brute, and as Polonius drew near the solar he shared with his children, he imagined the various, vicious ways in which he might slay the Danish monarch.

Inside he found Ophelia weeping in Laertes's arms. "How now, Ophelia?" he said. "What ails your sister, Laertes?"

At sixteen, Laertes was a head taller than his father and far more winsome than Polonius had ever been. "The King is sending Prince Hamlet to Wittenberg," he said, stroking his sister's chestnut hair.

Polonius clucked—a sound that fell between a throat-clearing and a cough. "Good riddance, I say! You are fortunate to be quit of him. The fruit doesn't fall far from the tree. Like father, like son."

Ophelia wept harder.

"I've told her she's better off," said Laertes. "Prince Hamlet's will is not his own. He is subject to his birth. Eventually, he'll have no choice but to leave her. But she believes she loves him. She has since we were children."

"Love!" cried Polonius, throwing his hands in the air. "What knows a maid of love? With a father who's been stripped of his post? His reputation? His status? Everything he's worked to build? What would your departed mother think of this display, Ophelia? You should be weeping for your father instead of that brutish Prince!"

"Oh my lord!" cried Ophelia, rising to her feet. "You will never understand!"

The girl fled. Laertes stood to follow, but Polonius laid a hand on his son's arm. "The King sends young Hamlet away?"

Laertes nodded. "To school in Wittenberg."

Polonius stroked his beard. "It's time you had an education, Laertes."

"Can we afford it?"

"You think me a spendthrift?" said Polonius. "You think I have put nothing aside? That I have no thought for the future?"

"Where would you have me go?"

Polonius paced. He meditated on the ideal setting for a quality classical education. A city drenched in culture—one from which fine art and philosophical ideals sprang forth, one to which all the best families flocked. A destination infinitely preferable to Wittenberg.

"Laertes!" he crowed at length, grasping his son's shoulder. "I will send you to Paris!"

The night before Prince Hamlet sailed for Wittenberg, the King hosted a masked ball in his honor. Elsinore was wound with garlands and multihued streamers. Fresh flowers bloomed in every corner, and white petals carpeted the flagstones. In the Great Hall, candles blazed from a hundred bronze candelabrums, and a band of musicians played the lute and the lyre. One lord dressed as a shepherd, his wife and children as his sheep. An earl disguised himself as a pasha. There were dozens of jesters, men laced into the elaborate gowns of their wives, and at least three courtiers dressed as the Danish King. King Hamlet himself attended as Fortinbras—he'd broken an arrow in half and affixed the pieces to either side of his head to mock the dead Norwegian monarch. Claudius, in the simple guise of a stable hand, spent most of the evening surreptitiously watching Queen Gertrude lavish affection on young Hamlet. As she danced with the boy and stroked his cheeks, Claudius's hostility mounted. The prince's presence had started pressing on him like a weight, shrouding him in constant gloom, and Claudius was relieved that he would soon be quit of the boy. He found himself wondering, as he watched Prince Hamlet kiss Gertrude's hand, why he felt no similar threat from the King. Why he felt no guilt over the blatant manner in which he'd cuckolded his own brother.

When the ball was in full session—when couples swung around the floor and wine flowed like blood from an open artery and laughter rang off the walls—Yorick the jester threw open the doors and bounded into the Great Hall. The fool was wrapped in bedclothes. He wore a false gray beard and wig. Under one arm he clutched a gander, and under the other a hen. Silence seeped through the chamber as he capered, assaulting lords and ladies, begging their forgiveness. The musicians ceased their play. The guests halted mid-swing. All eyes were pinned to the jester's birds. Poultry had not been seen at Elsinore in nearly thirty years, and the sight of the fowl had a strange effect on the attendees, who would later agree that a collective chill ran over them. That it seemed for a moment as though they'd spied two small, feathered ghosts.

Claudius stood across the hall from the dais on which King Hamlet sat beside Queen Gertrude. Yorick pranced—oblivious to the gravity of the scene—and Claudius knew that he should move forward, that he should stop the fool, but his feet were rooted to the flagstones. He and his brother had kept their pledge never to speak of the old King's death. There had since been no mention of poultry or poison or the souls of the Departed between them, and the sudden desire to observe the impact of the jester's pantomime on his brother burned a hole in Claudius. Prince Hamlet, dressed as a gravedigger, stepped out of the shadows—where he'd been whispering with Laertes and Ophelia—and crept toward the white-faced King, whose hands had clenched into fists. Yorick had doted on young Hamlet since the prince was a boy, and Claudius wondered if the Danish heir had orchestrated this performance. As the King rose, as he descended the steps of the dais and advanced on poor Yorick—who rewarded the squawking hen and honking gander with loud kisses—Claudius considered darting forward to seize the birds, to shield them from his brother's rage.

But when King Hamlet grabbed Yorick's shoulder, he did not strike the fool; he laughed heartily and congratulated him on his disguise. The King relieved the jester of the hen and the gander and held the birds aloft. "My fool has ended the ban on fowl at Elsinore!" he cried, and the Great Hall was choked with cheers, and the musicians struck up with renewed fervor. The guests took turns dancing with the birds, passing them from hand to hand. There was hungry talk of the culinary changes the King's proclamation would bring to

Elsinore—of succulent goose breast and tender duck legs; of custards and omelets; of sweet, rich cakes. Claudius watched Prince Hamlet, who'd retired to a corner with Yorick's gander, sit stroking the bird's white feathers, gazing into its flat black eyes.

The next morning the Danish heir set sail for Wittenberg. That night poor Yorick was discovered near Elsinore's gatehouse. His breastbone gleamed in the moon's pale fire. The fool had been torn open from pelvis to larynx.

## Act V

It was impossible to connect the body of Yorick—or any of the seventy-seven bodies discovered on the grounds of Elsinore over the next eight years—to King Hamlet. None of the killings was ever witnessed, no evidence discovered on any of the corpses. The victims were scullions and porters, chambermaids and grooms. An occasional courtier or councilor. Traveling merchants. An entire troupe of actors. Mostly, people who would not be missed. Claudius investigated these crimes, ignoring his suspicion that his brother was solely responsible. His brother, who'd grown more stooped and distracted since Prince Hamlet left for Wittenberg. Who'd come to rely on Claudius almost entirely for the day-to-day running of Elsinore and Denmark.

"My husband is a monster," Gertrude would say as she and Claudius toured the castle grounds, visiting trees against which he'd once pressed her to hike her skirts and explore her recesses. "He still comports himself like a berserker on the field of battle."

"There is no evidence against the King," Claudius would remind her.

"My lord," Gertrude would say, shaking her head. A smattering of white peppered her ginger hair, and tiny lines creased the skin around her eyes and mouth, but to Claudius she was lovelier than she'd been the day she approached Elsinore on her dappled mare. "Why cannot you take action?"

The reasons for his inaction were manifold. Hamlet was his brother as well as his King. Claudius feared any steps he took would be motivated in large part by his love of Gertrude. And there was young Hamlet, who would never believe his father had been irreparably damaged by the horrors of war, his own sins, a blood-borne curse, or a combination thereof. The prince would hold Claudius accountable and enact an overblown vendetta—he would turn their lives into a tragic farce. Claudius and Gertrude continued parading the grounds, approaching coops constructed eight years earlier when the ban on fowl had been lifted. The couple ducked inside one of these rank, wood-and-wire structures, where Claudius slid his hand beneath a hen, extracting a warm egg. He found another and placed the hen fruit in the white palms of the Queen. "Can you feel it?" he asked.

Gertrude nodded. "Life," said she.

"I have no interest in death," Claudius said.

"But what of your pact?" said Gertrude, gentle hands squeezing the eggshells. "Did you not swear that if your brother exhibited a sickness of mind, you would take care of him as you once took care of your father?"

There was a time when Claudius had been unable to hide anything from Gertrude, but he'd since learned to deceive and dissemble. The Queen knew nothing of the savage yearnings her own son had awakened in him. She had no idea that Claudius was increasingly plagued by foul dreams from which he would wake with a shriek, images of blood rivers and mass graves burned into his consciousness. That often, in the dead of night, he abandoned his bed for the stables of Elsinore, where he would mount the first lusty, unbroken stallion he found, driving the beast mercilessly over the Arcadian grounds, barking at the moon. That at times his fingers quivered so with the desire to tear and shred, to choke and gouge, that he could scarcely control them.

"My love," said he, "do not we all suffer from some form of madness?"

Gertrude stroked his cheek. "Not Claudius. Not my tender prince."

But he was unable to move against the Danish King until the day he came upon the list. Hunting for a deed among his brother's papers, he discovered—tightly rolled and pushed to the back of a drawer—a sheaf of parchment. Dozens of pages, covered front and back with cramped script. As Claudius carried the sheets to the window, his heart knocked around in his chest. His palms dampened. He let sunlight stream over the pages, and he saw that they were covered with names—hundreds of which had been marked through with a decisive stroke of black. Alone in the Chamber of State, Claudius's voice shook as he read aloud the words printed at the top of the first page: "Enemies of Denmark." He recognized the names of Norwegian commanders his brother had killed during the long-ago campaigns they fought as youths. He recognized the names of chambermaids and grooms who'd been found mutilated on the grounds of Elsinore. He saw the name *Yorick*. Near the end of the list, he saw Gertrude's name, and the name *Prince Hamlet*, and the name *Claudius*. His left hand twitched. His palm burned, and he studied the scar that traversed it.

"From this time forth," said he, "my thoughts be bloody, or be nothing worth."

In the library Claudius dug through volumes crammed on dusty shelves and towering upon counters until he located a worn alchemy text—one he'd last seen thirty-seven years earlier. As he exited the chamber, he nearly collided with Ophelia. The flower-faced maid, who once raced through the castle with young Hamlet, filling the stone corridors with frenetic life, had wilted since her father's demotion and the departure of the Danish heir. Poor Polonius, too—still aggrieved over his dismissal—now drifted through the halls of Elsinore like an unhappy spirit caught between the realms of the living and the dead.

"How now, Ophelia?" Claudius said.

"Well, my lord," said the girl, who pressed between her hands a slender volume of verse. "Do you know when Prince Hamlet returns from Wittenberg?"

"I'm sorry, my child," said Claudius. "I know not."

Disappointment clouded Ophelia's eager countenance, and Claudius was tempted to caress her cheeks. There was something infinitely appealing about the girl, who—at the same time—had always had a bit of doom hanging about her. When Claudius touched her face, Ophelia did not pull away. She trained her eyes on his, and he thought he read approval in her pellucid gaze.

"Can I be of assistance, my lord?" said she.

Prince Claudius shook his head, and Ophelia's heart broke for him, as it was common knowledge that he loved Queen Gertrude. Ophelia herself had fallen in love with Prince Hamlet when she was eight years old. She'd often prayed for some impediment to place itself between them, for she couldn't resist the idea of star-crossed love. Her father warned her against the prince, but that didn't count—her father warned her against everything. When Hamlet was sent to Wittenberg, however, Ophelia discovered the unwelcome pain of separation, and she now prayed fervently and nightly for his return. But poor Prince Claudius, who lived in such close proximity to the Queen, might as well have been separated from his lady by three oceans. Ophelia wondered if he knew that the profundity of both his love and his desolation was etched always into his face. If he realized that tears leaked from his eyes even now, as he touched her cheeks in the corridor outside the library.

"Dear child," said Claudius, "may God always keep and protect you."

As he moved through the forests surrounding Elsinore —searching out the black mushrooms he needed to concoct his deadly potion—Claudius fondled the warm duck eggs he'd slipped into his pockets. He tried to picture himself and his brother as frolicking boys, but he could imagine only young Hamlet and Polonius's children at play. He stood as the sun tumbled from the sky, thinking of the man who might or might not have been his father, silently entreating the old King's spirit to appear before him. But Claudius did not really expect to start seeing ghosts.

In his solar, he mixed ingredients carefully. He sat on

a stool, staring at the flagon of inky liquid, waiting for the dead of night. Once Elsinore was still, Claudius crept through dim corridors, ascending the stairs, passing tapestries and mounted weapons. The door of the royal solar slid open silently at the merest touch. He discovered his brother curled on his right side, cradling the sheaf of parchment listing the Enemies of Denmark. The King's breath whistled softly. As Claudius gazed down at the ruins of his brother, he was seized by the uncanny sensation that he was following a script. That he had no control over the steady hand emptying the flagon's contents into the ear of the Danish King. That the elation and gratification that buoyed him as he committed this second unforgivable act were not his own emotions but those he'd been instructed to evoke. "Your brother sends too many to the afterlife," the old King's spirit had said. But had the specter ever spoken? Had the ghost ever appeared at all?

As Claudius shook the last drop of poison from the flagon, his brother's eyes opened. Claudius leapt back. The flask clanged against the flagstones. Hamlet's mouth gaped, and his left arm shot out—hand open, palm up. The scar that crossed his life and fate lines seemed to Claudius to glow with an unnatural illumination. Without his consent, Claudius's own left hand rose and pressed itself to that of the King. "Death to all enemies of Denmark," gasped Hamlet. The last sound he made was not unlike the dying whimper of Radolf—the wolfhound he'd killed years earlier. When he expired, the sheets of parchment spilled, fanning over the flagstones.

The Lord Chamberlain discovered King Hamlet's body. The monarch had apparently slipped away in his sleep just as his father had before him, and at the same age. The man who'd bested Fortinbras—who'd kept Denmark secure and more than doubled her holdings—looked more peaceful in death than he ever had in life, and the Lord Chamberlain was struck by his youthful appearance. Years had been stripped away like old varnish. For the first time in ages, the Danish King looked like a boy. Before calling in porters to tend to the body, the Lord Chamberlain removed the unusual items he found clutched in the King's hands—two duck eggs, still warm to the touch.

Claudius was named King three days later. He pointed out that Prince Hamlet was next in line for the crown, but the Danish nobles wouldn't hear of it. It was rumored that young Fortinbras—son of the slain Norwegian king—was gathering forces with a vengeful eye toward Denmark, and Hamlet, who'd been studying in Wittenberg for nine years, was simply too inexperienced to step into a leadership position in a time of crisis.

They never discussed the mechanics of King Hamlet's death, but Gertrude assumed that Claudius took her husband's life. That he'd committed this act so that Claudius and Gertrude could live together as man and wife. Because he had, from the first moment he spied her, loved her. One month after the death of the King, they were married in a small ceremony at Elsinore. Polonius, whom Claudius had reinstated as Lord Chamberlain, Ophelia and Laertes—home from school in Paris—served as witnesses. Gertrude welcomed Claudius back into her bed, where they remained for three days. On the fourth morning, the Danish Queen woke dizzy with the knowledge that life once again brewed inside her. Claudius's seed had taken root in her womb.

The force of creation flowed from Gertrude, filling Elsinore, seeping into every chink and crevice. Claudius often affixed his lips to the Queen's still-flat belly, and the vitality brimming within her bolstered him—giving him strength. He massed forces against young Fortinbras and Norway, filling holes in the country's defenses. He allocated funds and deployed brigades and led councils and delivered inspirational addresses. Denmark was on the brink of war, but Claudius actually sighted contentment within his reach.

Then young Hamlet returned from Wittenberg.

As the prince entered the Great Hall with his schoolmate Horatio—as Queen Gertrude embraced her son, now grown into a man—Claudius was again struck by the eerie notion that this scene had been conceived of by another. That he was merely a character—one of many—being manipulated by some invisible hand. Hamlet greeted Laertes and Ophelia, but his gaze remained fixed on Claudius, casting a pall over the Danish King. Claudius forced himself to smile and clasp the prince in his arms, but accusations written in Hamlet's dark eyes enraged him, and blood thumped through his veins so loudly he wondered if others could discern it. "He's entitled to a measure of resentment," Gertrude said that night as she cradled Claudius's head in her lap. "You've been named King and married his mother. But things will soon settle down."

From that day forward, however, events tumbled one after the other with the surety of predestination. When Hamlet wasn't sulking, he behaved in an antic fashion—treating blameless Ophelia with scorn and derision. Gertrude worried that her son was suffering from hereditary madness, but Claudius suspected that the prince was acting. That he, like Claudius, had perceived the drama unfolding around them. It seemed to Claudius that Hamlet stank of rot and decay, and he wished to excise the prince from Elsinore—to remove the festering cancer of his person. He thought to send Hamlet to England, but Claudius entered the Great Hall one afternoon to find that a troupe of players had descended on the castle, and he knew the end was beginning.

"But, my lord," said Gertrude when Claudius attempted to dismiss the troupe, "it has been so long since we had players at Elsinore. And it seems to me a perfect distraction."

The play was called either *The Murder of Gonzago* or *The Mousetrap*, and as Claudius watched the nephew of a king pour poison into the king's ear and marry the king's wife, he stole glances at Hamlet, who lay at Ophelia's feet. Had the prince put the players up to this? Had he seen another ghost on the battlements of Elsinore? Had the spirit of King Hamlet revealed itself? Was his brother suffering in the afterlife—enduring torments at the hands of those he'd slaughtered?

Calling a halt to the performance, Claudius withdrew to his solar. He opened the chest in which he'd hidden his brother's list of Enemies of Denmark alongside the old King's yellowed inventory of the Departed. He pored over thousands of names, wondering if it made any difference that his own list was so much shorter. He thought of the Queen Mother—of how, at the end of her life, she'd finally learned to bend her stubborn knees. Of how much comfort she'd derived from her orisons. Claudius knelt and clasped his hands beneath his chin. When he closed his eyes, he saw the old King—bowing and begging the pardon of chickens and pheasants and geese. "Forgive me," he'd said. "All of you must forgive me." These words, however, would not come to Claudius's tongue. He did not know at whom to direct them. The old King? Hamlet the first? Hamlet the second? As Claudius knelt, prayerless, he thought of the heir burgeoning within the Danish Queen. For the first time, he understood that an unseen author had pitted Claudius and young Hamlet against one another contrapuntally. That there could be no resolution without one taking the life of the other. From here on, death would settle like a broody hen over Elsinore.

When Hamlet mistook Polonius for Claudius and ran the Lord Chamberlain through with a saber, as Polonius hid behind a tapestry in Queen Gertrude's solar, Claudius banished the prince to England carrying secret orders for his own execution. Doe-eyed Ophelia—driven to distraction by the death of her father at the hands of the man she loved—drowned in a weeping brook. The day she was interred in unconsecrated ground, a misty fog veiled Elsinore. Claudius stood at her graveside with his arm around weeping Gertrude. His hand rested on the shoulder of Laertes, recently arrived from Paris, who was still reeling from the shock of his father's slaying when word came of his sister's sad demise.

"Lay her in the earth," the boy said. "From her fair and unpolluted flesh may violets spring."

As the priest prayed for Ophelia's soul, Claudius envisioned the face he'd caressed outside the library of Elsinore.

Had the maid been tainted by the curse that hung like a blade over the Danish royal family? Had her doom been merely a matter of unlucky proximity? A squawk roused Claudius from his thoughts, and he turned toward the sound. Peering into thick mist, he spied small, feathered shapes stepping forward, shedding the cloak of fog. Three hens paraded through the graveyard in a funerary fashion. Behind them another shape materialized—one far larger. When Claudius recognized the form of Prince Hamlet, he gasped.

"They are coming," said Claudius. "The souls of the Departed."

But he had not learned to see specters. The prince had not been reborn; he'd escaped Claudius's death sentence. Hamlet leapt after Laertes into the yawning earth, and the grief-stricken men grappled in Ophelia's grave, arguing over who'd loved her more. In Laertes, Claudius identified a ready accomplice, and as he and the son of slain Polonius plotted the death of Hamlet, he recalled the prince in his scowling, impudent youth. He thought of how difficult it had been at times to prevent his hands from acting of their own accord—from bruising and bloodying the boy. Or running him through. Had he sensed even then that fate had set him against the Danish heir? As Claudius tipped a blade with poison, as he filled a failsafe goblet with tainted wine, he became convinced that he'd rehearsed these actions a thousand times and could perform them without benefit of sight. This knowledge assured Claudius, and a calm sense of conviction settled over him.

"This pleases me, my lord," Gertrude said when Claudius informed her that he'd arranged a fencing match between Hamlet and Laertes. "Though he resists you, you are the only father my son has known. It's time love sprang up between you."

In the Great Hall she sat beside Claudius, her white hand at rest on his knee. Here was the gentle man she loved—her husband at last. Here was her son, strong and fully grown. Inside her a new spark thrived—a child would be a product of love. As she watched Hamlet and Laertes parry and thrust over the floor of the Great Hall, surrounded by Danish courtiers, Gertrude was overwhelmed by joy such as she had never known. She wanted to laugh—to break into song, to act out the sort of unlikely scene that occurs only in a comedy. When Hamlet landed a second hit on Laertes, Gertrude rose and crossed to her son. She wiped his damp brow with her scarf. She offered him the wine her husband had poured, but Hamlet refused to drink.

"The Queen carouses to thy fortune," she said, lifting the goblet.

"Gertrude, do not drink," said Claudius.

But it was too late. The Queen sipped from the poisoned cup, and the nimbus of light that surrounded her began to flicker and fade. She resumed her seat and grasped Claudius's knee, but as the Danish King looked upon that white hand, it shriveled into a skin-wrapped claw. In place of Gertrude he saw a rotting corpse. A moan escaped his throat—a sound so full of despair that every head in the Great Hall swiveled in his direction. "How now, my lord?" said the Queen, pressing one hand to his cheek and the other to his forehead, but Claudius could not speak; he could scarcely breathe. Memories flooded him—Gertrude approaching Elsinore on her gray mare, Gertrude stepping from the shadows in the stables—and pain crushed him like an enormous fist. Yet the sight of the woman he loved clutching at her throat, gasping like a lamb born with underdeveloped lungs, seemed to Claudius nothing more than a scene out of a play. One that was proceeding rapidly to its conclusion.

"Oh, my dear Hamlet," said the Queen, "the drink! I am poison'd."

As she collapsed on the flagstones, the life force ebbed from the room—leaking out of doors and windows, emptying Elsinore of warmth and meaning. Both Hamlet and Laertes had been bitten by the poisoned blade, and Laertes confessed his treachery. "The King," said he, "the King's to blame." Hamlet advanced on Claudius, looking as spectral as his father and grandfather, and Claudius wondered how he'd mistaken a story so mired in blood for anything other than a tragedy. Could he truly have imagined a tale that opens with a patricide pivoting to end with a wedding or a birth?

Claudius reached into his pocket, extracting the duck egg he carried like a talisman. The ovoid token fit succinctly into his palm, and the Danish King closed his eyes—anticipating the undeniable pulse—but he felt nothing. Claudius examined the shell—that thin barrier that stands between hope and destruction. It seemed appropriate that he should take a moment before enacting his own death scene to deliver an internal soliloquy—one that connects the egg to the fleeting fragility of life. A monologue that ponders whether man makes choices or is acting always under the scripted aegis of fate. A discourse on the distance between the dead and the living, between truth and illusion, between sanity and madness. When Hamlet plunged the poisoned blade into Claudius's chest, Claudius cried, "Defend me!" but he expected no help. The phrase spilled from his lips like one he'd rehearsed and committed to memory. After Hamlet forced the remainder of the poisoned wine down Claudius's throat, the Danish King fell, facing Gertrude. Her image prompted him to deliver his ultimate line—the prayer he'd formerly been unable to utter.

"Forgive me," said Claudius as loudly as he was able, but not loudly enough for anyone else to hear. "All of you must forgive me."

A shiver passed over young Fortinbras as he prepared to enter the well-hewn halls of Elsinore. After routing the forces of Poland, the Norwegian prince had arrived in Denmark expecting to take the throne by force, but he discovered Elsinore undefended. Horatio—friend of Prince Hamlet—who along with the King and Queen lay lifeless on the rush-strewn floor of the Great Hall, presented Fortinbras with the Danish crown. Horatio recited a tale of murder, treachery, and vengeance—a tale of such woe, of such tragic proportions, that Fortinbras couldn't help suspecting that the man was prone to exaggeration.

As the Norwegian prince examined the golden circlet that had recently rested on the brow of Claudius, brother of the late King Hamlet, a white hen appeared in the Great Hall. The bird sought out Claudius's body—pecking at his nose and open eyes, scrambling onto his blood-soaked chest. Danish courtiers and Norwegian captains alike stood aghast. Another hen appeared, and another. A pheasant joined the chickens, and a goose, and a drake. Before long the Great Hall was teeming with poultry. The birds multiplied with astonishing rapidity, seeming to spring fully formed out of dead air. In the midst of the squawking, honking fracas, young Fortinbras spied strange things—flashes of featherless, flesh-toned skin, the malformed hand of a young Pole he'd recently killed in battle. A gander broke loose from its gang and waddled toward the Norwegian prince. In the bird's flat black eyes, Fortinbras read terrible accusations, and for an instant, he considered fleeing the halls of Elsinore. He considered finding a distant, barren mountaintop—a place to pass the rest of his appointed days in solitude, far from the means, motive, and opportunity to take the life of another.

"Good my lord," said Horatio, "Denmark awaits your command."

Shaking his head to clear the melancholy fog that had descended, Fortinbras ordered his captains to bury the Danish royal family. He ordered them to round up and butcher the birds—to mount their carcasses on spits over flames to feed the Norwegian forces. Later, after he'd toasted his troops and eaten his fill of fowl, young Fortinbras stood before a sea of soldiers on the grounds of Elsinore, silently summoning his father's ghost. When he placed the crown of Denmark upon his solemn brow, he found the thin circlet to be far heavier than he'd imagined.

# DEAR AHAB

Would that your harpoon-line hadn't coiled itself around your neck, that you hadn't been dragged into the shifting depths of the drink. Would that my skin had grown too thick to be pierced, that I'd never become entangled in your lines, that the *Pequod* had merely chased me over the wet hills and valleys of the Pacific like a playful dolphin and returned to Nantucket with all hands accounted for. I may lack reason—as Starbuck well knew—but that does not mean your hunger for vengeance was madness. You were right to seek it, for I was after you. To your mind I was a great white backdrop against which things stood in shadowed relief, a canvas onto which you could splash your vitriol and bitter hatred. You painted on me a cursed image, one representing every foul malignancy that exists under heaven. In spite of my size and might—in spite of my undeniable physicality—for you I dwelt not in three dimensions but in the cave-world of signs and symbols. To my simple eye, however, you were more than corporeal. You were shockingly real. After I bit off your leg at the knee, I couldn't stop thinking about you. I drifted—suspended in striated, moss-green depths—amid darting schools of fish and circling porpoises. As octopi and conch dragged themselves over the littered sea floor, I dreamed forever and constantly of you. *Ahab. Ahab. Ahab.* Wondering when the *Pequod* would sail, when she would carry you back to me. It wasn't that you were the first man I'd tasted. I'd eaten my share of whalers and had developed a thirst for the blood of man. Or not blood so much as fear. Or not fear so much as reason. There is something about the way a man shrieks as his flesh is torn and his bones splintered, about the way he begs and pleads. His capacity for reflection makes even instantaneous death a slow and incremental affair. But you, dear Ahab, uttered not a sound when I maimed you. You cried out neither to some loved one on earth nor to your God on high. You sat instead on the deck of your sinking ship, glowering, blood leaking from your stump to cloud the salty sea. Your calf whetted my appetite, but I didn't want to devour you at once. I fantasized about ingesting you piecemeal. Your left hand. Your right foot. A forearm. A chunk of abdomen. A portion of thigh. A shoulder. I envisioned stripping you—chipping away at your person until you were but a grimacing, cursing head. I thought I might stretch this process out, that the promise of breaking you down might sustain me. But in your fevered quest, you lashed yourself to me with stout ropes, and I unknowingly pulled you into depths from which man cannot resurface. Once I noticed your limp, lifeless form trailing me, I took you in my jaws and secreted you gently in a coral reef. Today, a few shreds of flesh cling to your polished bones. My efforts against whalers have grown feeble, and the world seems a tenebrous place—one devoid of promise. I glide through the Pacific, throwing a colossal shadow over the sea floor, wondering what volume of the ocean has been displaced by my tears.

# A MOMENT ON THE LIPS

*U*ntil the day that wily Achaean invaded my cave, I thought misery was an inevitable condition of existence. It was all I could do to haul myself vertical and roll the boulder out of the way each morning. The sunlight that drenched the rocky meadow where my flocks grazed seemed to me unnecessarily bright and oppressive. I wasted countless hours sitting with my chin in my hand and my eye on the ground. I rarely bathed, shaved, or changed my tunic. I yearned, but I couldn't put that yearning into words. I didn't even realize I was yearning.

"Polyphemus?"

I looked up from the boulder on which I slumped to find Loticleus standing before me. My sheep surrounded us, grazing on sparse tufts of grass. My goats wandered at a greater distance.

"Afternoon, Loticleus." I resumed staring at the ground, hoping he would clear off. He did not.

"What are you doing?"

"Tending my flocks," I said. "What does it look like?"

I guess I should point out that most Cyclopes aren't terribly bright. I don't mean to speak ill of my brethren, but it's true. And Loticleus is the dullest of us. It isn't that he can't put two and two together and come up with four; he can't even put two and two together. Loticleus's eye is the color of sheep shit, and it's always watering. At this time, he would tear out clumps of his own hair for no reason, and his beard was always full of brambles. He was by far the fattest Cyclops on our island—a craggy patch of land off the Sicilian coast. This was due primarily to his inability to stop eating his own sheep and goats, which he devoured at an absurd rate. Loticleus couldn't get the hang of pacing himself, and he never seemed to grasp that his animals needed time to reproduce. I'd heard that he'd eaten himself down to a handful of goats and two ewes, and saliva glistened on his slack lips as his eye roved over my flocks.

"I'm hungry, Polyphemus."

"No you're not. You just think you are."

"Guess what I ate yesterday."

"I can't imagine."

The lid descended over his eye, and one of his grimy hands rubbed the gut pushing out the front of his tunic. "A man."

"Bullshit."

"It's true!" Loticleus shouted, his lid flying up.

"You're lying." Even as I said it, I knew he wasn't. Loticleus isn't really capable of deception.

"NOOO!" he howled, stomping his filth-blackened feet. The ground trembled, and my startled sheep herded away from him.

"All right," I said. "Keep your tunic on."

"He washed up on shore clinging to a piece of driftwood," he said. "I bashed his head into the ground and ate him right there. I couldn't help myself. He was so tasty."

Unlike most Cyclopes, I had never partaken of man. Generally we subsist on a diet of sheep, goats, sheep and goat by-products, and any other warm-blooded creatures that stray into our paths. Local men avoid our island at all costs, but strangers sometimes land on its beaches, and shipwrecked men or those who've been put off sailing vessels occasionally wash ashore. My brethren claimed that man tasted far more pleasing than sheep or goat, but the thought of devouring a being that shares my shape—two legs, two arms, a torso, a head—and walks upright, even one with an eye on either side of its face, did not sit right with me. It made my heart convulse in a way I wasn't able to identify. I'd never been face to face with a man, but I was certain that if I were, eating him would be the furthest thing from my mind.

"What we need," Loticleus was saying, "is a great storm to drive aground all the ships within a thousand miles of the island. Then we could feast on men for days!"

I silently begged him to go away.

"What about your father?" he said.

"What about him?"

"Why don't you ask him to call up such a storm?"

I should probably point out that I was born of Poseidon and a Nereid named Thoosa, but the God of the Sea and I had always had a strained relationship. Whenever he stopped by my cave with his entourage of Naiads and Nereids, I would roll the rock in place and sit there holding my breath, pretending I wasn't home.

I stood. "Don't you think Poseidon has better things to do? Would he call up a storm just to fill your fat belly? Besides, when was the last time any of us paid attention to him? Made him a sacrifice or offering? You know how gods are—they aren't apt to do anything for anybody without something in return."

As Loticleus stood absorbing my words, I patted his shoulder and took my leave. I herded my flocks into the fenced yard and through the laurels that screened my cave. Once the most stubborn of my goats was inside, I used the boulder to seal out the world—welcoming the rank gloom of my home. Amid stony protrusions and hanging rock formations, I had constructed pens for my flocks. Milking pails crowded the dirt floor—some stacked into teetering towers, some half full of sheep's and goat's milk. Cheese stored in baskets overflowed the cave. The floor was littered with bones, hooves, and tufts of wool. In places, the sheep and goat shit was ankle deep. Dried brown blood splattered the walls like abstract cave art; here and there fresh red streaks glistened from the sheep I'd breakfasted on that morning.

My ewes and does bleated, so I sat on the milking stool. My flocks were abundant, and the task took me three hours. Once I'd deflated every udder in the cave, I sat in near darkness surrounded by full pails of milk. The round, dully glowing white disks put me in mind of the moon. I suffered from terrible insomnia—waking most nights with a start, struggling up through thick dread, my heart a-hammer. It always took me some time to realize there was nothing to fear. I was alone in my home surrounded by the warm, wool-covered bodies of animals who knew a contentment that hovered outside my reach.

Once awake and unable to quiet my mind, I would rise and make my way to the shore, relishing the sharp stones that perforated the soles of my bare feet. I would study the moon until its image dissolved in my monstrous tears. There was inside me a darkness far deeper than that of the firmament, and it grew unchecked like a cancer. My fellow Cyclopes seemed content with their solitary lives, but the lonely days of uncivilized brutality that stretched before me made me want to sleep the eternal sleep.

Sitting on the milking stool, I wept like one suffering a grievous injury. High-pitched whines. Freely flowing fluids. Choking sobs. The sort of display that should never be witnessed. Afterward I sat limp, feeling like a sheep's udder out of which I'd squeezed every last drop. I rose, collected sticks from a pile in a corner, and briskly rubbed two together. Igniting a small flame, I blew upon it until the twigs I'd mounded caught fire. I tried to focus on the fire's benefits—its light and heat—but as usual, my gaze was drawn to shadows the flames threw over the walls—menacing, unknowable. I chanced to drop my eye from the shadows to the cluttered cave floor; it was then that I caught sight of the men.

I'd only seen men from afar and suspected that their minuteness had to do with perspective, but no—these men were far smaller than I'd imagined. Rejected by Galatea, a Nereid with whom I once become violently infatuated, I killed her lover—a man named Acis—by flinging a rock at him from a great distance. When my anger subsided, I was flooded with a shame that now resurfaced as I realized how miniscule the men crouching behind milking pails and baskets of cheese and bloody piles of sheep and goat bones truly were.

"How dare you?" This wasn't what I wanted to say, but the words erupted from me, shaking the cave walls. I was shocked and taken aback, especially as I considered the great blubbering display I'd just put on—one the small strangers had no doubt observed. But I wasn't angered by their presence. They seemed to me tender, miniature, two-eyed Cyclopes, and at the sight of them I was filled not with rage but with something unfamiliar and equally warm. I longed to wish them welcome.

I tried again, but my tongue continued to betray me. "Who are you? How did you come here?"

A man whose muscles filled out his tunic and whose golden hair and beard curled lyrically—a man I now know to have been Odysseus—stepped forth. Placing  hands on hips, he squared his shoulders with a tiny show of bravado. "If you please, we are weary soldiers, followers of Agamemnon, blown off course on our way home from the sack of Troy. We ask in the name of great Zeus—who guards strangers and suppliants—that you give us food and shelter."

"Zeus be damned!" I thundered, meaning, *I would offer you food and shelter even if Zeus didn't look after strangers and suppliants.* Seeing what a terrifying impact my voice had, I continued as softly and calmly as I could. "What I mean to say is, I don't give a damn about Zeus."

I could tell they still weren't taking my meaning, and I was about to explain how lucky they were to have wandered into *my* cave rather than the cave of the man-hungry Loticleus, when out of the corner of my eye I noticed two of them sitting in a basket of cheese, cramming their faces full of the white stuff. I was warmed by the sight of them enjoying something I'd made with my own hands—something I'd never before had the opportunity to share—and I reached out, plucked them from the basket. Still chewing, they struggled and kicked in my grasp. Their companions shouted, pleading with me to release their friends. Dangling the men before my eye, I realized that, though essentially structured like Cyclopes, they were in truth much comelier. Their bodily proportions seemed more harmonious. Also, their eyes were almond-shaped—like the eyes of beasts.

"I order you to release my comrades!" Golden-haired, muscular Odysseus stomped his little foot as he commanded me so. I was going to obey, but instead I did something that, at the time, I could neither explain nor understand—I slapped the two men against the cave floor. Their heads split open, and their brains soaked the ground. Tearing them limb from limb, I devoured them—organs, flesh, and marrowy bones—then washed them down with three pails of sheep's milk.

The ten remaining strangers fell to their knees or prostrated themselves on the shit-covered ground. They wept and screamed and tore their beards and flailed around in grief and horror. I licked traces of their fellows from my fingers, trying to determine what had compelled me to do such a thing. I had not been angry—far from it. From the moment I touched the men, I was flooded with a feeling more tender than any I ever felt for the Nereid Galatea. I had for a split second imagined holding them forever, yet I was compelled to beat them into the floor and devour every part of them.

Ashamed—unable to look the men in their tiny animal eyes—I withdrew to the far side of the cave. I stretched out among my sheep and goats, where I pretended to sleep. Sometime in the night, one of the men—Odysseus I am sure—stole across the cave. I felt the tip of his sword poke my sternum, but so miserable was I, that I did not brush it away. A short time later I heard him sob and curse softly, and the sword was removed.

After dozing fitfully for an hour, I arose—determined to make a fresh start with the men. I'd spent the night trying to reconcile my vicious behavior with the warm tingle that moved through me whenever I thought of the petite, perfectly formed beings imprisoned in my cave, but I could not. Disgusted by what I'd done, I only knew that I would never—under any circumstances—eat a man again. As I milked my ewes and does, I felt the small strangers eyeing me, and I tried to think of something to say that would assure them they had nothing more to fear.

I had a speech all planned out but had only gotten as far as "Listen, men. Should I call you men? Is there something else I should call you?" when my hand shot out of its own volition and snatched up two more of them. Before I knew what I was doing, I'd smashed their little skulls into the ground and gobbled them up. My head whirled with the speed of it. The eight survivors stared at me agape. I belched, and the flavor of their companions flooded my mouth. I wanted to be sickened by it—to detest it—but the truth is, my fellow Cyclopes were right. Man *does* taste far more pleasing than sheep or goat.

Odysseus and his crew once again prostrated themselves—lamenting and tearing their hair, imploring great Zeus to help them—and I considered rolling the rock aside and allowing them to escape. But as I watched their heartfelt display of grief, I knew that I could not. Not only would Loticleus and the other Cyclopes eat them, but if I let the men go, they would never get the chance to know me.

For after I'd eaten the second set of them—while their blood and juices still glistened on my chin—it struck me that I loved them. The men were precious and pleasing to my eye, and I loved them, and I wanted them to love me—I *needed* them to love me. I no longer knew if their flesh was truly sweet or if it just tasted so due to the love I bore them. Love crashed down upon me like a heavenly hammer, making my former infatuation with Galatea look like a meaningless crush.

I wanted to explain all this, but I'm no good at extemporaneous speeches. If I collected my thoughts and put together the right words, I felt sure I could make them understand why I'd eaten their friends. It had nothing to do with hunger or anger or vicious brutality. I hoped that if I made this clear, they would forgive me and consent to remain in my cave as my companions forever.

So I said nothing. I rolled the rock aside and drove my flocks out through the laurel-covered cave entrance. Once the animals were outside, I faced the men—who stood shin-deep in sheep and goat shit, blinking up at me in terror and anguish. Before sealing them inside, I wanted to flash them a reassuring smile—one that said all would be explained when I returned—but I was afraid a bit of their comrades might be stuck in my teeth.

I rapidly covered the sun-soaked ground that stretched between my cave and the meadow. At one point I started skipping. My sheep and goats eyed me askance, as if the dumb beasts were wondering what had come over their master.

"Polyphemus?" Loticleus stood slack-jawed in the meadow, scratching his crotch. Nearby two ewes and four bony goats grazed. "Great Zeus, is that you whistling?"

Apparently I was also whistling.

"I suppose so." Closing my eye, I tilted my face up to the sun. "How does this lovely day find you, Loticleus?"

"Hungry."

I laughed—a clear, deep sound I had no recollection of heretofore making.

"What's come over you, Polyphemus? I've never seen you in such a mood."

Shrugging, I settled on a boulder. "Have you eaten yourself down to this?" I asked, indicating his pitiful animals.

Loticleus nodded. "I don't know what will become of me. I suppose I'll starve."

I agreed. It did seem the most likely outcome.

"What about those men?" Loticleus said.

I leapt to my feet. "What men?"

"The men on ships. Ships you could ask Poseidon to run aground on our island. If only you would, pitiful Loticleus might not starve."

As a rule Cyclopes don't bother with compassion, and his attempt at arousing it in me was another mark of his idiocy. But Loticleus had caught me on the right day. My eye roved over my abundant flocks, and I made him an offer. "If you promise to give them a chance to start reproducing before you devour them, I will give you twenty sheep and twenty goats."

"Give?" So unheard of was such generosity among our brethren that Loticleus did not understand what I meant.

"They will be yours. They will belong to you."

His shit-colored eye brimmed with tears. He yanked up the hem of his tunic to dry them.

I touched his shoulder. "Soon you will have your own abundant flocks."

Loticleus departed with his new sheep and goats, and I paced the meadow, considering what to say to the men in my cave, who were no doubt cowering in fear. I would explain that it had never been my intention to eat any of them, and that I would do so no more. After all, if I continued devouring them, they could not become my companions, and it was this above all else that I desired.

Once I'd herded my flocks inside and replaced the boulder, I positioned myself as far from the eight remaining men as I could. Their sleepless faces bore a hunted look. Fear clouded the air between us, making me want to weep. I started pacing nervously, and as I did so, I kicked something sharp. Buried beneath sheep and goat shit, I discovered a pole I intended to use as a herding staff. One end had been sharpened to a fine point—something I did not remember doing—but I didn't think too much about it. Tossing the pole aside, I swung around to pace in the opposite direction, and when I was within arm's length of the clustered men, I grabbed two of them, dashed them headfirst into the floor, and ate them.

As I sat on a stone, hiding my face in my hands—aghast—I felt a tap on my knee. I looked up, and golden-haired Odysseus stood before me. In his hands was a bowl of thick, black liquid.

"Oh great Cyclops," he said, "take this wine to wash down the flesh of my comrades. It is the finest my ships carry."

I was speechless. Despite my behavior, the little man was

offering me libation. Deeply touched, I took the vessel and drained it. The drink was sweet and strong. As soon as I emptied the bowl, he filled it again. And again.

"Tell me," I said, my words slurring, "what is your name?" In my foggy vision, Odysseus seemed cloaked in mist and clouds, a bit of heavenly stuff—a miniature god. So busy was I with thoughts of picking him up and cradling him—of placing him on my shoulder and letting him ride there forever—that I did not hear his reply. I wanted to assure him that I would never eat him, but the wine tricked my tongue, and I mumbled something else entirely before darkness swept over me like a tide called up by Poseidon, and I collapsed on my back.

In vivid dreams brought on by Odysseus's wine, the island's colors were brightened, its lithic landscape made lush. Gazing upon my reflection in a clear pool, I found that my eye had been replaced by two almond-shaped eyes—one situated on either side of my face. Delighted, I scoured the verdant terrain for the men, who hid from me not out of fear, but for a lark. Even those I'd already devoured were there—sprung back to life. When I discovered each man, he did not scream; he congratulated me, and I placed him on my shoulders amidst his fellows. With my new eyes I saw each strand of hair on his precious head, each bead of sweat that stood upon his sun-darkened skin.

Agony jolted me—searing, unbearable. Awake, I leapt to my feet. My eye was open, but I saw nothing. Touching my face, I discovered a narrow object protruding from the center of my crackling, sizzling, popping eyeball. I yanked on this item and heard a sucking sound followed by the gurgle of thick liquid. Once the object was in my hands, I recognized the sharpened pole I'd previously kicked. I flailed around the cave—running hither and yon in fright-ful darkness. My screams must have painted the air, hang-ing like a portrait of anguish for those who still possessed the power of sight.

"Polyphemus?"

Voices floated to me from outside the cave.

"Why are you screaming?"

I lurched forward. My hands landed on the boulder that covered the mouth of my cave.

"Is someone stealing your sheep, Polyphemus? Is someone harming you?"

I recognized the voices of Loticleus and others. Sounds of violence and pain are not uncommon on our island, and I realized how bloodcurdling my screams must have been to bring my brethren on the run.

"Polyphemus?"

Pain hummed and thumped through me. In an act of will worthy of an immortal, I managed to silence my screams. A metallic taste filled my mouth; blood and other fluids had been flowing to it from my punctured eyeball. I spit on the floor and steadied my voice.

"Nobody is here. Nobody is stealing my sheep. Nobody is harming me."

I heard one of my brethren suggest that great Zeus had sent a sickness upon me—one that had driven me out of my mind. Afraid of contracting it, my fellow Cyclopes departed, remarking that I should call upon my father for help.

I bumbled around, touching every inch of the cave, but now that I was blind, the men could easily avoid me. I kept grabbing bleating sheep and goats. I wanted to explain to the small strangers that I'd told my fellow Cyclopes nobody was hurting me in order to protect them—to assure them that I would let no more harm befall them—but instead I barked things like, "It's no use hiding! I can smell your fear!"

Finally I rolled the rock aside and sat in the cave entrance with my arms outstretched. It would be impossible for the men to pass without my notice. As I sat in the chill night air—quaking with pain, drying blood stiffening my beard and tunic—I realized my fellow Cyclopes were right. Great Zeus *had* sent a sickness upon me. Not the literal darkness in which I now found myself adrift, but the melancholy that had tainted all the previous days of my life.

When my ewes and does began bleating to be milked, I knew day was dawning. The rams and billy goats crowded the cave entrance, but before letting them pass, I felt the back of each for a man sitting astride him. As I ran my hands over the last ram—the best and fattest I owned—my fingertips brushed something foreign on his underside. I knew instantly that Odysseus was clinging to the ram from beneath, and that his remaining companions had been clinging to the others. I was tempted to snatch up the muscular, golden-haired man and force him to remain with me, but I knew it was no use. In the end I would only devour him. Calling upon reserves of restraint I did not discover until I lost my vision, I allowed my best ram to wander from the cave.

A short time later shouts reached my ears, and I blundered toward the sea. I stumbled, falling to my knees again and again. Rocks and stones gashed my flesh. When water lapped at my ankles, I stood with my head cocked, listening to Odysseus, who used a new voice—one raised in triumph from the prow of his ship.

"For eating guests in your home, you have been punished by great Zeus, oh Cyclops, with the loss of your livestock and your sight!"

I heard the thunder of my fellow Cyclopes approaching. I felt them staring at my obliterated eye—at the blood staining my flesh and tunic. I picked up a colossal stone, heaved it wide of Odysseus's voice, and held my breath. When the little man laughed and shouted, relief flowed through me.

"If any man asks who blinded you, tell him it was Odysseus—son of Laertes, sacker of cities, who makes his home in Ithaca!"

Again I felt the weight of my brethren's stares, and I knew they were thinking of the prophecy. A Cyclops named Telemos had once foretold my blinding at the hands of one called Odysseus, but being so caught up in my melancholy, I'd all but forgotten his prediction. Its fulfillment made me acutely aware of the power of the gods and of my own limitations; however, I felt no more anger toward the miniscule hero than I had before I learned his identity.

I knew my fellow Cyclopes were waiting for me to retaliate, so I lifted my arms to the heavens, and for the first time in a decade I spoke to my father. I asked Poseidon to prevent Odysseus from reaching his home. If he *did* see Ithaca again, I asked that he be late, lose all his comrades, and find trouble in his household. Considering how strained things were between us, I doubted that my father would heed my prayer, and it was just as well—for no matter how Odysseus had abused me, I could think of him with nothing but love.

I grabbed another boulder and heaved it in the direction of his ship. To my relief, my brethren told me I'd missed again. Mumbling condolences, they departed, and soon I thought myself alone on the rocky beach.

"Polyphemus?" Loticleus's rough hand landed on my shoulder. "They took your flocks?"

"The males. I've still got the ewes and does. I'll have to use the males I gave you to rebuild."

Loticleus was silent.

"How many of the animals have you eaten?"

"Several."

"How many?"

"Quite a few."

"How many?"

"All but ten!"

I was shocked. "You ate thirty animals in one day? How is that even possible?"

"I'm sorry," he sobbed. "I couldn't help myself!"

Loticleus had always seemed to me nothing more than a moronic eating machine, but I now understand his compulsion to consume. It isn't about hunger or gluttony or even boredom—it's about love. About inviting what you love inside. Making it a part of you. Ensuring that it remains with you forever.

We put the remaining male animals to work impregnating my does and ewes, and our shared flocks are now abundant. Loticleus has moved into my cave, and he acts as my eye. The responsibility has done wonders for him—he takes better care of himself and no longer devours animals at such an alarming rate. When I now wake in the night, I have only to reach out and touch his warm, slumbering shape to feel assured by his company. I've actually grown fond of Loticleus—something that comes more easily when one can't see him. But my feelings will never match the consumptive love I still bear the tiny men who invaded my cave and took my sight—six of whom I carry inside me. My eternal companions.

# PENNY DREADFUL

When the sparkling, well-bred girls tease you for being an orphan, for having a mother who overdosed on laudanum and a father who took his own life, for being a charity case and scrawny and descended from the Romanies, when they shove you in the yard of the boarding school or scald you in the showers, do not cry. Do not let them know they've touched you in any way. At night, when they are sleeping, indulge in subtle revenge. Release clicking carrion beetles and cursorial wolf spiders between their sheets. Replace their shampoo with lard. Dunk their toothbrushes in the toilet. They will suspect you. They will accuse you, but if you are careful—if you are smart—they won't be able to prove a thing. The headmistress will never believe one so meek could plot and carry out such machinations. When she dismisses the charges, do not smile. Learn to conceal your emotions. This ability will serve you well.

Read everything you can get your hands on. Literary masterworks and serial mysteries, romantic novels and sci-fi thrillers, pulp magazines and penny dreadfuls. Become obsessed with gutsy, glamorous heroines—women who buck convention and blaze trails and break hearts. Make top marks in every subject, marks that unfortunately will get you nowhere. You will be no beauty and have no connections or prospects. Upon graduating, you'll have a choice— take a position caring for an affluent widower's daughter clear across the country, or join your aunt, who works in the school kitchens, slaving for hundreds of the same girls who've made the last nine years of your life miserable. Do not think twice. Take the position.

Anticipate hating the child, but find her to be nothing like the wealthy girls you've known. From your first glimpse of her astride a stygian stallion named Mephisto—a horse far too big for an eight-year-old to handle—you'll become intrigued. Watch her bring the beast in line, digging into its flanks with spurs affixed to her little heels, flogging it with a crop, driving it around a course set up behind the widower's country estate. Watch her black hair stream, her muscles tense, as she leads Mephisto into one jump after another. "It's no use telling her to be careful," her father will say, glancing up from the business section of the *Times*, sipping scotch. "It's no use telling Rebecca anything."

She will possess more wit, nerve, and spirit than any adult you've encountered—this child in your charge—and though ten years your junior, she will become your first actual friend. Together you will concoct clandestine games and hold late-night séances and recite famous tragedies and perform original dance routines. She'll confess deeds, hopes, and fantasies that should scandalize you but won't. Allow her to bewitch you as she bewitches all who cross her path. Do not consider revealing her secrets to her remote father, who will be terminally away on business, managing to miss every milestone, every equestrian competition and sailboat race. Enjoy the honor of being her co-conspirator. Collect her shed clothing, and when no one is looking, bury your face in each finely crafted article. Inhale her pure ambrosial scent. Buff her pink skin with a washcloth. Brush her dusky hair—one hundred strokes a night. Weather her tumultuous tantrums for the joy of watching the sun break over her once again.

On her insistence, take a husband. The man who runs the stables on the estate. Pretend this situation suits you. Put off performing your wifely duties for as long as possible, and when he finally locks the door and forces himself on you, leave your body. Float away. Watch your little lady sleeping peacefully in her canopied bed. Until he finishes, dream of living with her on a sprawled country estate, in a monumental Tudor-style manor house perched precipitously on sea cliffs. When she asks you about sex, lie. Tell her things you've only read in pulp novelettes and penny dreadfuls. "Oh Danny," she'll say, her inky eyes glinting, "I can't wait until I'm old enough to make love!" Two weeks before your tenth wedding anniversary, your husband will be kicked by a spooked horse. Once he dies from his injuries, conceal your relief. Conceal your glee. Start dressing all in black.

At sixteen your lady will start sleeping with stable hands on her father's estate; men she meets in department stores and at her boating club; her cousin, Jack. Help her hide this. Help her juggle her lovers—all of whom are fated to fall for her, to lose their heads. Secret yourself in the shadows of her boudoir or a barn or a boathouse as she forces her opalescent body against a wide assortment of sinewy men—as she attacks them like a starved, carnivorous animal—and feel your heart tighten with a concoction of jealousy, admiration, and love.

Do not be surprised when at twenty-four she announces her engagement to one of the country's wealthiest bachelors, and do not expect her matrimonial intentions to change her behavior. "I'll live as I please, Danny," she'll say repeatedly until the day before she dies. "The world won't stop me." While she and her husband honeymoon in Monte Carlo, it will be up to you to pack her trousseau and travel to the West Country estate on which you'll spend the next eleven years of your life. The lorry will wind around a tree-lined drive for more than a mile before the dense vegetation recedes and you catch your first glimpse of the house. Do not gasp. Do not cry out. Though you won't have ever seen Manderley—not even a picture postcard—you'll recognize from your dreams the decorative half-timbering, the oriel windows, the gabled roof, the abundant chimneys of the Tudor-style manor house perched precipitously on sea cliffs, and you'll recall something your mother said before she sank forever into the soft bosom of laudanum: "Getting what you wish for, my darling, has its own set of difficulties."

Embrace the elegance, the spaciousness, the unequivocal grandeur of your new home. Prepare for your lady's arrival by taking the other servants in hand. Ignore their palpable resentment. Tighten the household until it hums. When your lady returns from Monte Carlo and says, "You've done a bang-up job, Danny," swell with pride. Allow yourself to believe that your mother might have been mistaken. That it might be possible to live happily ever after in this house overlooking the sea.

Notice how the husband stares at your lady—as though she is a malevolent specter, a sanguinary monster who eats unsuspecting children—and understand that she has revealed to him her true nature. There is no chance, however, of him giving her away. He won't risk the scandal; name and reputation mean too much to him. He and your lady are destined to present a portrait of wedded bliss to the world as she renovates Manderley—hosting masked balls and soirees, transforming the house into the most celebrated, most visited home in all of England.

Whenever the bars of her gilded cage close in on your lady, she's sure to relieve the pressure by tempting fate. She'll sail alone on tempestuous seas in a yawl named not *Millicent* for the mother she never knew, nor *Minerva* for the wise goddess, but for her girlhood stallion *Mephisto*. To escape, she'll take frequent trips to London. While she's away, busy yourself with the running of the household. Try not to worry. Draw her bath as soon as she returns. Kneeling beside the tub, scrub her pink skin as you did when she was a girl. Listen to the details of her trysts, of sex with multiple partners, of how far her cousin Jack can shove his fist inside her. You'll often wonder why she shares these things with you. If she needs another in whom to store her many sins. Will she understand that it excites you—listening to her exploits while washing her body? That you lie awake at night in the room connected to hers, listening to the even sound of her breath, envisioning the scenes she's painted, your fingers fumbling between your thighs?

A decade into her marriage, your lady is bound to grow careless. The stream of men who visit her seaside cottage will upset the husband, but she'll shrug and say, "What's it got to do with you?" When he hurls insults at her—when he accuses her of being less than human—shield her with your body. Note how thin she looks, how weary. Tuck her into bed and watch her sleep. Try not to spend every waking moment fretting about your indomitable lady, who will appear—for the first time in her robust life—to be breakable.

One stormy night, she will take *Mephisto* out alone, and she will not return. Before the call comes, before the husband drives up the coast to identify a body, you'll understand that she is gone. Ignore the voices clamoring in your head. Do not plummet into the void your lady once filled. Though your heart will be torn asunder, do not follow your father's example. No sitting fully clothed in a tepid bath. No straight razor pressed to your wrists. Try not to think of the woman to whom you've dedicated your life—the woman who could not stop tempting fate. Never show the husband or the rest of the staff what your lady's death has drained from you. Keep her things just as they were when she touched them last—the furs and gowns and jewels, the brushes and silk scarves and bottles of perfume and lotion, her china ornaments and Renaissance paintings, her roses. In this manner, preserve her. Sustain her memory. Conjure her ghost.

When the husband cables from Monte Carlo less than a year after her death to announce that he's married a girl young enough to be his daughter, reach back to your school days. Reacquaint yourself with revenge. The new wife will be a mousy, awkward thing—the complete antithesis of your lady. Decide that you despise her, but when you confront this usurper for the first time, you'll find that she touches something deep inside you. Her obvious confusion and discomfort are sure to remind you of a lonely orphan at a faraway boarding school. Do not let this sway you.

Think always of your lady, and how this pretender is trying to take her place.

Make things as difficult as possible for the would-be replacement. Never miss a chance to point out her inadequacy—to make her look like a fool. Remind her of the superiority of your lady. Present her with evidence that the husband could never love another. When she breaks a china cupid in the Morning Room, make her feel like an ignorant child. Watch her squirm, and try to take pleasure in her discomfort, but you'll find that you cannot. Despite your undying love for your lady, her proxy will inspire more pity than contempt. Conceal the tender sentiments aroused by the pretender's inability to hide her thoughts and feelings—by her complete lack of guile. You're certain to find yourself musing about what might have been if you'd met under different circumstances. If you'd reached simultaneously for the same stream-of-consciousness satire or historical potboiler in a bookstore. If, over coffee in a small café, she'd revealed to you that her parents also died tragically. Pointlessly. If you'd discovered that she, too, had been an outcast. That an even playing field stretched between you.

Begin to question whether your lady ever thought of you as more than a servant—an automaton designed to pick up after her and buoy her constantly with admiration. As more than a repository for the burden of her sins. When you start neglecting the care of her things, it will feel as though the bedrock beneath your life has shifted, turned to sand. Fight to keep your emotions in check. After a slew of sleepless nights, you'll conclude that in order to remain loyal to your lady, you must rid yourself of the new mistress of Manderley.

Devise a scheme that involves a fancy dress ball. Convince the pretender to wear, unwittingly, the same costume your lady once wore. Count on the fact that the inevitably unfavorable comparisons—the embarrassment and the shame—will be more than the mousy girl can handle. When she confronts you in your lady's bedroom the day after the ball, you'll long to put your arms around her. To comfort her. To cover her plain face with kisses. Ignore these impulses. Instead, attempt to talk her into ending her own life. It is the only way you can maintain allegiance to the spirit of your lady. Despite how much it pains you, lead the pretender to the window. Push aside the curtain and throw up the sash. Watch the fog roll in. Say, "What's the use of staying here? You're not happy. Your husband doesn't love you. Why don't you jump? Why don't you try?"

She's not destined to jump, however. At that moment, a cargo ship will run aground on the sea cliffs. When men dive down to investigate the wreckage, they'll discover a second sunken boat—a yawl with a body inside, a yawl upon whose stern *Mephisto* will be painted in bold red strokes. Knowing she sailed alone the night she died, you'll realize the body the husband identified a year earlier couldn't have been that of your lady. Your lady is still trapped on the seafloor.

When it is revealed that *Mephisto* was willfully sunk, a coroner's inquest will be ordered. A verdict of suicide will be returned, but your lady's cousin—Jack of the penetrating fist—is sure to challenge this ruling. He'll claim that your lady was pregnant with his child. That she was murdered by the husband. He'll bring a police official to Manderley and ask you to lie about your lady.

"She was not in love with you," you'll say instead, "or with Mr. de Winter. She was not in love with anyone. She despised men."

"Didn't she come through the woods to meet me night after night?" Jack will say. "Didn't she spend the weekends with me in London?"

"And what if she did? Lovemaking was a game with her, only a game!" Once you start revealing the truth, you'll find yourself unable to stop. "She did it because it made her laugh. She laughed at you like she did at the rest!"

"Mrs. Danvers," the police official will say, "can you think of any reason why Mrs. de Winter would have taken her own life?"

Fight to maintain your composure. "No." Shake your head, clutch at your dress. "No, never."

But alas, you're doomed to break down in front of the official and the husband and the pretender—who will stand blinking her kind brown eyes and shaking her head, covering her mouth with one plain hand. You're fated to weep for your lady and for her replacement and for your parents. To weep for the first time since the age of nine.

When it comes out that your lady wasn't pregnant— that she was dying of cancer—the husband and the second Mrs. de Winter will be in London. Take advantage of their absence. Infiltrate every corner of Manderley. Wine cellars. Ballrooms. Gloomy attics. Water closets. Solariums. Breakfast nooks and dining halls. The indoor pool. The Morning Room. Wander the grounds and gardens. Stand atop cliffs. As the sun scorches a path to the sea, let the salt-spray coat your skin. Gaze into swirling, turbulent waters. Your lady's thinness and fatigue weren't figments of your imagination. Picture her in the seaside cottage, taunting the husband with her false, adulterous pregnancy. Hear her mocking laughter. Envision the husband producing a pistol and shooting her through the heart, just as she intended. See him rolling her in a rug, dragging her to *Mephisto*, sailing from the cove, drilling holes in the hull, opening the sea cocks. As you reconstruct the narrative of your lady's death—as you decipher the riddle, as you solve the crime—feel at once absolved and utterly abandoned. Bereft of the hand that has been pulling your strings. Freed from fate. Discharged from destiny. As though for the first time, it's up to you to write the next chapter of your life.

Briefly, entertain the notion of staying on at Manderley, tending to the new mistress as you once tended to your lady. Bathing her. Caring for her things. Living at her beck and call. You'll soon realize, however, that this is impossible. That the husband has only kept you around out of fear. So as not to arouse your suspicions. That the story in which you've been a supporting player has reached its resolution. Your services are no longer required. You'll be asked to leave as soon as the happy couple returns from London.

Reenter the grand house overlooking the sea. Float up the stairs to your lady's rooms. Touch her things. When you bury your face in them, however, you're bound to notice they've lost her pure, ambrosial scent. Even surrounded by the possessions of the first Mrs. de Winter—even in this shrine to her memory—you'll be able to picture only the brown eyes of her replacement.

Gather your few possessions. Retrieve a can of kerosene from the storerooms. Lock yourself in. Soak everything— furs, duvet, canopy, dressing table, jewelry boxes. Strike a match. Watch it burn yellow before tossing it onto a Persian rug. Stretch out on your lady's mattress. Feel flames waltz around you. Her sanctum will swiftly become stygian—an inferno ruled by Beelzebub or Mephisto. Do not act as your lady's avenging angel. Do not annihilate out of hatred, or for the wanton sake of destruction. Instead, use fire to wipe out past, present, and fated projection. To clear a swath, scorch the earth, burn things back to a tabula rasa. A starting point. For the husband and both the Mrs. de Winters. For a cook at a girl's boarding school. For a laudanum addict and a suicide. For a scrawny orphan girl, huddled under blankets with a flashlight and a penny dreadful, dreaming of treachery, obsession, and illicit love. Imagining a house perched on sea cliffs. Listening for the stealthy approach of a sparkling, well-bred girl named *Rebecca*.

# TIGERS DON'T APOLOGIZE

Mrs. Rosen's lengthy neck, sharp chin, and startled expression reminded Mowgli of an Indian crane. Jocelyn, who when they met had been soft and yielding like a sloth bear but was now taut and lean like a leopard, strained forward beside him on her miniature orange chair, and Mowgli half-feared that at any moment, his wife would bound across the desk to pounce on the elementary school principal.

"Oliver," Mowgli said for the tenth time, "cut that out."

But his son, whose birth six years earlier had plunged Jocelyn into a depressive state from which Mowgli had thought she might never emerge, refused to cut it out. Oliver crouched in a corner of Mrs. Rosen's office, snarling, growling, waggling his head. Occasionally he lifted a small, filthy hand to swipe at the air.

"I just don't see what the big deal is," Jocelyn said, her voice rising. "He's pretending. Kids do that."

"But Oliver refuses to *stop* pretending," said Mrs. Rosen. "He pretends during nap time. He pretends when the other children are finger painting and reciting the alphabet. He's been pretending since your husband dropped him off on the first day of school. In fact, no one here has actually met Oliver. We've only been introduced to Chaircon."

"Shere Khan," said Jocelyn.

"What?"

"The name is Shere Khan. Oliver can't pronounce it correctly. Shere Khan was a tiger. He stalked my husband when he was a kid."

The principal cocked her head. She blinked rapidly.

"You'll have to forgive my wife," Mowgli said. "She forgets how much of a shock it can be to learn that I grew up in the wilds of India."

"You're not serious."

He nodded. "Raised by wolves, I'm afraid."

Mrs. Rosen shifted her gaze to Oliver, who'd curled up and was licking his ankle. "We may not be equipped to deal with your son," she said. "Have you looked into special schools?"

"He can't be the first kid to have trouble adjusting," said Jocelyn.

"The boy's going through a phase," said Mowgli. "Six months ago he claimed to be a rhino. All summer he slithered around on his belly, insisting he was a python."

The principal pursed her lips. "His behavior is disruptive and distracting."

Mowgli glanced at Jocelyn, who might as well have been baring her teeth. "We'll talk to him," he said. "By Monday, Oliver will be ready to behave like a normal little boy."

As he steered the Volvo toward Valdosta Circle, Mowgli studied his son in the rearview. The boy roared ferociously. He gnawed on the leather seats. "Please stop, Oliver," Mowgli said. "Why are you doing that?"

"'Cause I'm Chaircon! Rawr!"

Jocelyn touched Mowgli's arm. "You know talking to him does no good."

"We'll try again." Mowgli glanced at his wife, whose worry lines had deepened with each pound she lost. "Stop fretting, Jocelyn. The man-cub will be fine."

"Maybe we should have waited until he was older to tell him about your childhood," Jocelyn said. "Or maybe we never should have told him. Maybe we should have said you were raised by potato farmers in Idaho."

But Mowgli had grown up believing things about his own

parentage that turned out to be completely fictional, and as a result, he'd vowed never to lie to his son. He dropped his family at the end of the drive and watched Oliver gambol across the lawn on all fours. Fallen leaves obscured the grass. The boy threw himself down on the golden carpet and thrashed around. Jocelyn stood watching Oliver, one hand shielding her eyes from the fierce light of the sun.

"Are you two going to be OK?" Mowgli called through the open window.

Jocelyn nodded. She waved him on.

Mowgli watched his wife shrink in the rearview, and he wondered what went on when he wasn't around. Jocelyn's depression had rendered her unable to care for Oliver after his birth, so Mowgli had been forced to step in. Having had no human infancy of his own, he'd treated Oliver like a wolf cub—nuzzling and stroking the boy; bathing him with his tongue; curling around him at night; making soft, growling sounds of comfort. Oliver was sixteen months old before Jocelyn was finally ready to mother. She attributed her recovery to an exercise and diet regimen her therapist helped her put together—a program that resulted in a transformation so radical Mowgli had trouble adjusting. Jocelyn insisted she'd never been happier, but Mowgli missed the soft girl he'd first noticed sitting in the back row of a night school Business Administration course. Jocelyn was pretty, but Mowgli—whose upbringing had heightened his sense of smell to a preternatural degree—was most drawn to her scent. It put him in mind of newborn fawns, young meerkats, newly hatched tailorbirds—tender, defenseless creatures he'd known in the wild.

As Jocelyn's body diminished and hardened, her scent changed. The vulnerability he'd found so appealing seemed to evaporate, and his wife took over Oliver's rearing with the ferocity of a lioness. Mowgli stepped aside, but at times he missed the closeness he'd shared with the infant Oliver. Now, as he drove toward Creature Comfort, the veterinary pharmaceutical company where he worked as a regional sales manager—a situation for which Mowgli, having spent

his boyhood among feral animals, was uniquely qualified—
he wondered if Oliver's obsession with Shere Khan had
anything to do with the way Mowgli had treated his son
during the first months of Oliver's life.

That afternoon, Doug Jones took Mowgli to lunch. Doug
had been a salesman at Creature Comfort for less than a year.
Slope-shouldered and shaggy-haired, he was given to hye-
na-like giggling. At a large, communal table in a Japanese
steakhouse, Doug ordered a bottle of hot sake.

"None for me," Mowgli said. "I never drink at lunch."

"Come on, Boss." Doug giggled. "Live a little."

Mowgli had one sake and then another. Before he knew
it, he was telling Doug about the meeting with Oliver's principal.

"Unbelievable," Doug Jones said. "I mean, he's a kid.
Kids pretend to be animals. What could be more normal?"

"My point exactly," said Mowgli. He watched a chef
squirt oil across the grill. Flames leapt up. The chef flipped
a shrimp in the air. Caught it on top of his hat.

"So what about this Shere Khan?" Doug Jones said.
"Are you telling me you actually killed a Bengal tiger when
you were eleven years old?"

Mowgli nodded. "He'd been stalking me since I was
a baby."

"Damn!" Doug exclaimed, pouring another round of
sake. "You are one serious badass!"

Mowgli drank. "Not really," he said. "It was him or me.
It's like that in the wild."

Some time later, Doug Jones steered the conversation
around to Creature Comfort's sagging sales figures. "I
know I'm still the new kid on the block," he said, "but I
also know the company's in the red, and I have some ideas
about how to get us into the black."

Mowgli smiled at Doug, who'd taken on the endear-
ing qualities of an ocelot. A blurry one. "I'd love to hear
them," he said.

"The first thing we need to do is tackle the big accounts,
make sure our customers are truly satisfied, make sure

we're moving as many antibiotics, steroids, and tranquilizers as possible. I know the Lake Park Zoo account is one you handle, but I noticed those numbers are down across the board, and I was wondering if you'd mind me taking a peek at the file. Maybe I could sit in on Monday's meeting. Look at the situation with fresh eyes."

Mowgli clapped a hand on Doug's shoulder. "Be my guest, Doug Jones!"

He'd only eaten half his chicken teriyaki when the room started spinning. Doug helped him outside, where Mowgli vomited into the koi pond.

After work Mowgli found his wife prowling the den, a gauze bandage wrapped around her forearm. The soft girl from the back row of the Business Administration course would have launched herself at his neck and clung to him. Jocelyn merely worried her lip with her incisors. "Oliver," she said. "He bit me."

Mowgli was still a bit woozy from his lunch with Doug Jones, but he quickly sobered. He led Jocelyn to the couch. "How bad is it?"

She shrugged. "I'll live."

They sat, and Mowgli unwound the bandage. He'd been raised on raw flesh—jockeying for position beside fresh kills, separating meat from bone with teeth and nails as warm gore dangled from his chin—but the wet crimson ring on the underside of his wife's arm made his stomach lurch. Unlike the mark of a wolf, Oliver's bite was a nearly perfect circle.

"Jesus."

"It's not so bad," Jocelyn said, rising and continuing to pace like a caged panther.

"What happened?"

"I tried to talk to him about school, to explain that we need him to stop being Shere Khan, to go back to being Oliver. I tried to hug him, and he bit me."

"Why didn't you call?"

"We didn't need you." Jocelyn stopped in front of the

window. She folded her arms, staring past the golden leaves that glinted like antique currency in the descendent sun. "I'm not helpless, you know."

"Did you spank him?"

His wife turned. She shook her head. "I bit him back."

After Jocelyn departed for an eight-mile run, Mowgli rapped on his son's bedroom door. He received a snarl in response. Inside, he found Oliver crouched between the dresser and the wall, spitting and clawing. As a boy Mowgli had seen his wolf brothers nip thousands of times at Raksha, the she-wolf who raised him. Raksha would tolerate the behavior for only so long before retaliating. He smoothed out his son's mongoose-and-cobra-print bedspread and sat, wondering why Jocelyn had responded to their son like a she-wolf instead of a human mother.

"Daddy is upset with you, Oliver."

"Rawr!"

"You can't go around biting people."

"Rawr!"

"Why did you do it?"

"I'm Chaircon!"

"You are *not* Shere Khan. Shere Khan died in India a long time ago. He was a bad tiger, a mean tiger. Daddy had to kill Shere Khan or he would have eaten Daddy. Why would you want to be such a mean old tiger?"

"I'm not mean and bad! I'm just doing what comes natural to a tiger!"

Mowgli leaned forward, examined his son closely. "Who told you that? Who told you to say that?"

"Nobody! Rawr! I'm Chaircon!"

Mowgli watched his son gnaw on his own knee. At Oliver's age, Mowgli had been nothing but matted hair and sun-dark skin stretched over muscle and bone. He'd spent his days swinging naked on vines and hunting with the pack, climbing trees and foraging for sustenance. Oliver was just a regular kid, and the knowledge of how quickly he would be torn apart in the wild had always frightened Mowgli. But they didn't live in the jungle; they lived in a ranch house on Valdosta Circle, and it was up to Mowgli to teach Oliver the laws of man—to show him what boys did and did not do.

"When Mommy gets home, I want you to apologize," Mowgli said. "I want you to hug her and give her a kiss."

"Tigers don't hug and kiss! Rawr! And they don't apologize!"

Mowgli stood. His son emitted a guttural growl—one that originated deep in his throat. As Mowgli stepped toward the boy, Oliver came out of his corner like a rabid rhesus monkey—fingers flying, teeth bared, emitting an ear-splitting yowl. He flew at Mowgli with such wild fury that Mowgli stumbled backward, collapsing onto the bed. He hadn't felt so powerless since Bagheera the melanistic panther sat him down and confirmed Tabaqui the jackal's claim that Mowgli wasn't a wolf at all. That he was, in fact, a man.

That night Mowgli woke to a sound he knew but could not place. It was a droning purr—a hum—one that filled the air like a fog of locusts. He sat up, but he couldn't tell from which direction the sound came. He had to find its source, and Mowgli swung his feet to the carpet. Halfway down the hall, he identified the purr as one tigers use to confuse and bewilder men sleeping in the open—a sound that makes travelers and wanderers run straight into the mouth of the beast. He hadn't heard it since he'd left the Indian jungle. It enveloped his home like the buzz of cicadas, and Mowgli was overwhelmed by other sounds, sounds that stepped forward from memory—the rustle of long grass, the scratching of bats' claws, the hooting of owls, the splashing of fishes in pools. He saw a hard brown boy climbing trees for honey and swinging through the jungle. He recalled crouching in low branches on warm nights, spying on the huts of villagers, wondering about the men who set traps in the underbrush and had no fear of fire.

Mowgli opened his son's bedroom door to find Oliver sitting on his knees in the middle of the bed, gazing through the open window. When the boy turned his head, the humming purr ceased. Mowgli could just make out the glow of his son's eyes and teeth.

"I make a good tiger sound, don't I, Daddy?" said the man-cub.

On Saturday morning, Jocelyn made blueberry waffles. Mowgli didn't tell her about the sound their son had continued making throughout the night—the droning hum that prevented Mowgli from finding his way back into slumber. Oliver had always loved waffles, but the boy growled and knocked his plate to the linoleum.

"What do you want, Oliver?" Jocelyn said. "Mommy will make you anything."

"Rawr! I want raw meat!"

"Absolutely not," said Mowgli. He looked to his wife for corroboration but was surprised to find her glaring at him. "You cannot eat raw meat, Oliver."

"That's what I want! Rawr!"

Later, Mowgli washed the breakfast dishes while Jocelyn dried. Through the window over the sink, he watched his son patrol the backyard on his hands and knees. He couldn't remember the last time he'd seen the boy walk upright. Mowgli had tolerated Oliver's previous animal incarnations, knowing his son would eventually tire of such games and shift his attention to distractions of a different stripe. But seeing Oliver so enthusiastically adopt the persona of the tiger who'd dedicated himself to Mowgli's destruction was off-putting. Mowgli kept thinking of how, in the wild, when the Pack Leader grows too old to govern, the younger males set upon him and tear him to shreds.

"You think he'll be alright, don't you?" he said to Jocelyn.

"Of course," she growled. "I won't let anything happen to the man-cub."

As Mowgli drove toward Creature Comfort an hour later, he turned up the radio, trying to drown out the memory of Oliver's droning purr. Whenever Mowgli had heard the sound as a boy, he'd known his life was in jeopardy; still, in the end, it was *he* who bested Shere Khan. He used his reason to kill the lame tiger, then draped Shere Khan's skin over the wolf pack Council Rock. These human actions proved to his animal brethren that though Mowgli had spent his entire life among them, he could never really belong to their world. Mowgli had been forced to join the society of man, but he'd never gotten over his banishment. At times he found himself wishing he hadn't taken Shere Khan's life. That instead he'd been ingested by the tiger so that his remains might, at least, have rested in the wilds he would always think of as home.

As Mowgli approached Creature Comfort's main entrance, Phil—a round security guard with enormous glasses and ruffled brown hair—fluttered up from his desk and opened the door. "Mowgli?" Phil's magnified eyes blinked behind his corrective lenses. "What are you doing here on a Saturday?"

"I meet with the Lake Park Zoo people Monday," Mowgli said, "and I forgot to bring home the file."

But the Lake Park file was missing. Holding its place in his filing cabinet was a pink post-it note on which Doug Jones had written *See you at the meeting, Boss!* Remembering what transpired at the Japanese steakhouse, Mowgli groaned. He stood and made his way to Doug Jones's office. He let himself in and switched on the light. He scoured papers and folders on the desk and in the drawers, but he found no trace of the Lake Park file. He did, however, find a loaded top-secret prototype of a semi-automatic tranquilizer dart rifle tucked between the file cabinet and the wall. Intending to turn the illicit weapon over to Phil, Mowgli fished it out and walked back toward the building's entrance, where the security guard stood. Lifted his hands in mock surrender. "I give up." Phil grinned. "You got me."

Creatures in the wild often employ camouflage and misdirection in the name of survival, but Mowgli had never grown accustomed to the distinctly human art of deception. Instead of handing over the rifle, he winked. Pressed a finger to his lips. "Field testing," he said.

Phil nodded. He asked no questions.

Mowgli drove toward Valdosta Circle, glancing into the Volvo's passenger seat at the blue Creature Comfort windbreaker in which he'd wrapped the dart rifle. As he slid to a stop before his home, apprehension pinned him to the leather upholstery—the sort of feeling that, in the jungle, would have alerted him to the proximity of a predator. He opened the front door and stowed the gun in the hall closet before making his presence known.

"Jocelyn?" he said. "Oliver?"

"In here." His wife's voice was bright. He found her on the couch in the den. Oliver lay curled in her lap, sleeping.

"I don't believe it," he said. "What did you do?"

Her face dimmed. "What makes you think I did something?"

He sat and reached for his son. He felt Jocelyn stiffen.

"Mowgli . . ."

He noticed a dark speck on Oliver's chin. He touched the discoloration—it was rough and rigid. Mowgli scratched at the boy's skin, and the stain fell away in tiny flakes. "Tell me that's not what I think it is," he said.

"He wouldn't eat anything else," said Jocelyn. "But look at him now."

"Jocelyn!" Mowgli shook his head. "We can't feed the boy raw meat."

"You grew up eating it."

"I thought I was a wolf."

"Oliver thinks he's a tiger."

"It's not the same thing. He has *us* to guide him. I didn't know any better."

His son stirred. He blinked. Jocelyn stroked the boy's head.

"Oliver isn't an animal, Jocelyn. I think he needs to see a doctor."

"Rawr!" his son roared. "I'll kill Mowgli if it's the last thing I do!"

Mowgli scooted to the far end of the couch. "He just threatened to kill me, Jocelyn."

But his wife said nothing. She was busy scratching the man-cub under the chin.

◆  ◆  ◆

When he woke in the night, Mowgli sensed that he was being watched. Years had passed since he'd lived the kind of vigilant life that had kept him alive in the jungle, but vestiges of his upbringing remained. Traces of instinct he'd never been able to shake. A humming purr filled the bedroom, and a slight weight pressed him into the mattress. Mowgli didn't have to open his eyes to know that Oliver's face hovered above his—that his son's small teeth were bared, his nostrils flaring.

Mowgli sat up, shoving the boy off the bed. With the speed of a striking raptor, he bounded up and crouched over Oliver, pinning him to the carpet. Mowgli hadn't made such movements in nearly thirty years, but they were automatic, involuntary. He threw back his head, and a mournful howl escaped him.

Seconds later, he was yanked to his feet and slammed against the wall. His gaunt wife advanced on him until he could count the lines etched into her face. The pungent, protective scent his wolf-mother Raksha had emitted whenever her cubs were threatened rolled off Jocelyn in waves. "Don't lay another hand on the man-cub," she said, her teeth glistening in silver moonlight. She cradled the snarling boy and stalked from the room. Mowgli's tension evaporated, and he sank to the floor. He spent the rest of the night there— hugging his knees, wondering how he'd ever imagined that he'd successfully made the transition from animal to man.

Sunday morning, Mowgli found Jocelyn curled around Oliver in the boy's twin bed. He pulled on a flannel, retrieved the rake from the backyard shed, and raked the front lawn into golden piles of leaves. Once he'd entered the society of man, Mowgli had carefully observed the males of his species, and he'd attempted to follow their lead. He put himself through night school working as a busboy. He met and married a soft girl. He got a job in sales and bought a house. He had a son. He worked at least fifty hours a week. He tried to keep his clients and bosses and underlings happy.

He voted in local elections. He bought Girl Scout cookies. He mowed his yard. Once, he'd cheated on Jocelyn at a veterinary pharmaceutical convention, but he was so drunk he couldn't recall the sex. What he did remember was the guilt. Not guilt over letting his wife down—guilt over letting mankind down.

Animal relations had been so straightforward, but Mowgli had never figured out the intricacies of human bonds. This had much to do with what he'd missed out on—parenting, the shared culture of television and film, fashion and slang that would have infused the years during which his consciousness was forming in a jungle half a world away. He'd been with Jocelyn ten years, yet he'd never understood her. Through trial and error, he'd learned the proper responses to her queries and the most effective ways to approach her, but he'd never put together a map of his wife's emotions. Though he'd shorn his matted hair and hidden his sun-dark nakedness beneath business suits, khakis, and polo shirts, Mowgli had only been able to offer his family the kind of love that exists between beasts. Because he'd never *himself* understood them, he hadn't effectively conveyed to his son the laws of man. As he studied the golden piles of leaves dotting the front lawn of the house on Valdosta Circle, Mowgli knew he was responsible for the movements both Oliver and Jocelyn were making toward the bestial.

Certain that he would be ambushed at any moment, Mowgli slunk through his home, glancing over both shoulders. He dug through Jocelyn's files until he found the home phone number of her therapist, Dr. Gregory, the man who'd brought her back from the brink after Oliver's birth. He called the doctor and explained the situation. Dr. Gregory agreed to see Mowgli and Oliver first thing Monday morning.

"I'm so pleased to finally meet you, Mowgli," Dr. Gregory said some fifteen minutes into their conversation. "Your unorthodox boyhood is of great interest to a man in my line of work."

The doctor's head, chin, and lengthy arms were furred in

orangutan-orange. He sat on a blue chair across from Mowgli, who also sat on a blue chair. To Mowgli, even the doctor's furnishings seemed designed to soothe and comfort.

"I'm sorry Oliver bit you," Mowgli said. "He bit Jocelyn a couple of days ago."

Dr. Gregory glanced at his left hand, marked by the same crimson circle Mowgli had seen on his wife. "Comes with the territory," the doctor said. "I've given the boy a mild sedative. It should wear off in a couple of hours."

Oliver—who looked tiny and defenseless—lay stretched on a blue couch across the room.

"And where is Jocelyn?" said Dr. Gregory.

"She doesn't know we're here," Mowgli said. "I'm worried about her. She's been encouraging the boy. Feeding him raw meat."

"I see," said the doctor. "When did Oliver start playing the part of Shere Khan?"

"Two weeks ago. That's when he started kindergarten."

"So perhaps he's hiding behind the persona of this tiger to deal with his own fear of the unknown. The unfamiliar."

Mowgli shook his head. "Shere Khan was a coward. In India, man was considered the weakest and most defenseless of all living things. Not only was it unsportsmanlike to kill him, it went against the law of the jungle."

"Did you explain that to Oliver?"

"Yes."

"So he knows he's adopted the persona of a villain. Of a creature that actively hunted you. Wished to harm you."

"To kill me," said Mowgli. "Oliver wants to kill me, too."

"Why would your son want to kill you?"

"I've failed him," Mowgli said. "Him and Jocelyn. I've never managed to leave the jungle behind. Not really, anyway."

Dr. Gregory assured Mowgli that Oliver didn't actually wish to kill him. He retrieved his desk calendar and scheduled an appointment for Mowgli's family the following afternoon. Once he'd closed the book, Dr. Gregory crossed one leg over the other. Extending his long arms, he clasped his hands around his knee.

"Mowgli," he said, shaking his ginger head, "I'm struck by the irony of this situation. What if your son has grown up thinking he's a boy, when he's actually a Bengal tiger?"

"Jocelyn?"

Mowgli received no answer. Standing in the front hall—holding Oliver's limp body—he was reminded of the intimacy he'd once shared with his newborn son, of how close they'd been before Jocelyn thrust herself between them. In the den, he sat on the couch. He curled around Oliver, nuzzling the boy's neck and shoulders, stroking his limbs, making growling sounds of comfort.

With his son cradled on his lap, Mowgli picked up the phone. He spoke to Beverly—the receptionist at Creature Comfort—who informed him that he'd missed the meeting with the Lake Park Zoo people.

"I don't understand," he said. "That meeting's not until 2:30 p.m."

"Doug Jones rescheduled it for 8:00 a.m.," said Beverly. "Apparently his presentation blew Bob Futterman and Kiki Schmeltzer away. They've agreed to double their standing order for antibiotics and steroids. And triple their tranquilizer dart order."

"Jesus."

"Doug's taking over the Lake Park account."

"I see."

"Oh, Mowgli." Beverly's voice descended to a sympathetic tone. "Doug Jones can be a real snake."

Mowgli hung up. He was tempted to jump into the Volvo and drive to Creature Comfort. To tear aside his clothes and reveal the sun-dark former man-cub that lurked beneath his business suit. He was tempted to beat his breast, to brandish a sharpened stick, to challenge Doug Jones. But Mowgli's heart wouldn't have been in it. He thought of Akela, who'd led the pack while Mowgli was growing up, and how every wolf—including Akela—knew his reign had come to an end when he failed, for the first time, to bring down a sambhur buck during the hunt. Akela had been a fine leader of wolves, but in truth, Mowgli had never been more than a mediocre manager of pharmaceutical salesmen. Too civilized to scratch and claw for survival. Too primitive to interpret the handwriting on the wall.

Mowgli carried Oliver into the boy's bedroom. He stood beside the bed, studying his son's shaggy hair, his dark skin, his filthy hands and knees. Mowgli had never forgotten the devastating day on which he'd realized the ugly, furless creature that blinked up at him from still pools of water was his own reflection. From that time forward, there'd been no denying his otherness. If Oliver hadn't been born with the same face, Mowgli would never have learned to appreciate it.

He smelled Jocelyn's fierce, feral scent before he saw her. She stood in the doorframe, the prototype dart rifle he'd brought home from Creature Comfort wedged into her shoulder. One eye closed, she sighted him along the barrel. "What have you done?" she growled.

"He's fine," Mowgli said. His wife held the rifle like a natural extension of her muscular body, and he wondered where she'd learned to handle it. "Dr. Gregory gave him a sedative."

"Put the man-cub on the bed," she said, "and step away."

Slowly—regretfully—he did as she ordered. Oliver was coming around—the boy twitched and moaned. Mowgli let his hand linger on his son's cheek. "Jocelyn," he said, straightening up, but before he could apologize—before he could take sole responsibility for their son's crisis of identity—a tranquilizer dart hit him in the shoulder, spinning him toward his wife, who hit him with two more in the chest.

The drug stampeded through his system, and he cried out as the solidity of his surroundings crumbled. The carpet beneath his feet became a cushion of rustling grasses and rotting vegetation. The room's ceiling gave way to an impenetrable canopy of leaves, branches, and vines. Mowgli staggered around like a wounded wildebeest, clutching at model airplanes and picture books and army men as they dissolved into tropical blooms and colossal insects and ripe, dangling clumps of fruit. Jungle noises swelled—hoots and splashes and cries of warning, pain, and welcome. A fallen log had taken the place of his son's twin bed. Draped over it was a Bengal tiger.

Mowgli's stomach knotted. He knew killing the beast would put him on equal footing with the men who set traps in the jungle and had no fear of fire, the villagers whose huts he'd spent countless hours watching. He also knew that once he'd killed the tiger, there would be no going back to the only life he'd ever known. He crouched, ready to spring, yet as Shere Khan slunk forward—as the tiger's droning purr filled the night—Mowgli felt the earth reeling in reverse, back to an age before firearms, an age when creatures with four legs stood a chance against those with two. He caught the tiger's eye, and in its yellow-green depths, Mowgli spied a spark of kinship, of fellow feeling. As he fell to his knees, as he lifted his head, exposing his throat to his lifelong nemesis, to the object of his antipathy as well as his affection—his own son and heir—Mowgli understood that he was never a man. That he was, after all this time, still an animal. His killing of Shere Khan had upset the frail balance of nature, and it was with satisfaction—as well as wonder—that Mowgli now assumed his rightful position.

Long live the man-cub.

# TINY BONES

*I*t started with a boy named Wilhelm. I was staying with his family long, long ago when a great dearth fell upon the land. Like the famines of my youth, this dearth felt interminable and seemed, in many ways, to redefine want. There was neither a crust of bread nor a glop of gruel to be had, and as the dearth wore on—day in and day out—as Wilhelm's family and I grew weak and delirious with hunger, we were eventually unable to rise from our beds and remained supine from sunup to sundown, dreaming of sustenance and slowly but surely starving to death.

Wilhelm's father made a living cutting wood, and his modest cottage had a limited number of beds, so I was forced to share with Wilhelm—a small and rather sickly eleven-year-old, a bundle of nerves and awkward energy with thick spectacles and oversized feet. The boy snorted when he laughed and cried at the slightest provocation, and I often caught his father—a brawny outdoorsman—staring at Wilhelm, his expression mingling consternation and disappointment with something approaching hatred. I myself grew fond of the boy during the months we spent huddled under thin blankets, trying not to think of the gnawing in our guts. Before Wilhelm, I hadn't had much experience with children—in truth, I was rather frightened of them—but balancing on the brink of death leads to intimacy, and Wilhelm and I often held one another and wept long into the night. He was a great one for making up sentimental songs and doing silly voices, and if I'd been denied these distractions—distractions for which, if his father caught him, he would be yanked from bed and backhanded—desperate pathways might have opened to my mind. I should have done something; I should have tried to protect Wilhelm, but the woodcutter was an undeniable figure of authority, and I was a guest in his home— an unmarried cousin, a spinster, a burden—and felt that I had no right. Moreover, what happened to Wilhelm makes any such regrets beside the point.

When I say *what happened to Wilhelm*, I really mean to say what we did to him—his father and I, and his two sisters and, yes, even his own mother. What we did as the months wore on, as we all grew dull and listless, living on nothing but tepid water, breadcrumbs, and distant memories of nourishment. Wilhelm, who was—as I have perhaps already stated—rather sickly, started one afternoon breathing raggedly and sweating, and there were no more songs or silly voices, just the boy, now a collection of bones held together by membranous, vein-mapped skin. He stared with unblinking eyes—eyes that seemed to follow me like those of certain oil paintings. When Wilhelm's breath grew more labored and his gaze more intensely disconcerting, I called for his father, who dragged himself out of bed and staggered across the room. He looked down at the boy and placed a calloused paw on Wilhelm's forehead. The gesture was the most tender I'd ever seen the woodcutter make, and my eyes fogged, and I realized that even the most seemingly immovable man is capable of tapping into the deep well of feeling that joins us all, as members of the human race. Even a man who, for instance, abandons at the altar a girl of twenty in whose belly his seed has taken root, her head covered by a handmade lace shawl—the only surviving memento of her mother. When I wiped my eyes, I saw that Wilhelm's father had shifted his hand. It now covered the boy's mouth and nose. Wilhelm's bony limbs twitched under the bedclothes, and his fingers grasped weakly at mine, and then he grew still. It was a stillness I'd witnessed only once before. A stillness that spoke of permanence. Of finality.

"The boy is dead," Wilhelm's father announced to the room at large while fixing me with a look that said the manner of his death was something I would disclose at my own peril. Using reserves of strength I never would have guessed at, I pushed away from Wilhelm's body and to my feet. Wilhelm's mother and sisters rose from their beds and stumbled over, and we all stood staring down at Wilhelm's stillness. I was crying, but none of the others shed a tear. After a time, Wilhelm's mother sighed and said they might as well get started.

"Get started with what?" I asked.

No one answered. Wilhelm's father lifted the boy from our bed and carried him to the rickety dining table, his head dangling pitifully from his neck. His mother rattled around in the kitchen, pulling out knives and utensils, and the two girls tripped from the cottage to draw water from the well.

"What are you going to do?" I asked, my voice aquiver, the outside edge of awareness breaking over me.

The woodcutter's murderous fingers dug into my shoulders. "It is the only way."

I am almost sure I whimpered.

"If we do not, we will all be as dead as Wilhelm."

I wrenched myself from his grasp and fled the cottage, nearly colliding with Wilhelm's sisters, who hauled a tub of water between them. I tried to run but was too weak to cover much ground. The cottage stood in a clearing in the midst of an ancient forest, and just within the tree line, at the base of a silver maple, I collapsed on the snow-covered ground. Dampness seeped through my threadbare nightgown. I decided that I would lie there until the world faded away, that perhaps if I hurried I could catch poor Wilhelm and we could journey together—discover the waiting mysteries of the afterlife. Perhaps I would find what should have been my family there. Perhaps Albrecht would be waiting with open arms. Perhaps he'd been prevented from reaching the altar by a fatal accident and not some other woman after all. He'd once said only death could separate us.

At some point I woke in darkness. I was shaking violently, but I managed to struggle to my feet. I stood only a dozen yards from the woodcutter's cottage. Smoke rose from the chimney, and there was a smell—one that was not particularly good but made my mouth water all the same. I found my legs carrying me back, my hand reaching for the doorknob. Despite the direction my life has taken—despite the sins I have committed since—I am still shamed by what I did that night. I suppose in my own defense I can say only this: the instinct for self-preservation, in my experience, is almost impossible to ignore.

It turned out that Wilhelm wasn't the first child the family had eaten. Like Wilhelm, the woodcutter said with a pointed look at me, their eldest boy had died of malnourishment during a dearth ten years earlier, and there had been no sense in the rest of them starving as well. Even the infant Wilhelm—then only a year old—had partaken of the flesh of his brother, mashed into a paste and spooned between his full pink lips. It was a matter of survival, the woodcutter insisted, but afterward I was never the same. I thought Albrecht had stolen all my innocence when I was a girl, but the scrap that remained was obliterated by eating Wilhelm, a piece of whom lodged in my throat—a piece I was never able to clear away.

As soon as the dearth lifted, I left the cottage of the woodcutter, finding work in a pastry shoppe not far from the ancient forest. My mother had instructed me in the baking arts when I was a girl, and after she died in the dearth of my sixteenth year, I supported myself designing and building structures from lebkuchen or *hutzelbrot* or stollen, edifices accented with bonbons and *süßigkeiten*. Castles with moats and ramparts. Sprawling country villas. French chateaux. It was one such creation that brought Albrecht and me together. A storm was gathering the day he strode into the bakery and demanded to know who was responsible for the grand *kletzenbrot* manor house on display in the window. I was nineteen, and as clichéd as it sounds, I saw his gleaming boots and trim hips, his mottled gray eyes— eyes that seemed cut from the brooding sky that crackled outside the bakery window—and I was lost. When he asked me to construct a lebkuchen model of his family's estate, heat surged through me, pinking my cheeks. The wings of a dozen swifts whirred inside my rib cage. Before the year was out, we were betrothed.

Now, far older but no wiser, I once again took up the creation of pfefferkuchen monuments and soaring *striezel* towers. I worked twelve-hour days in the bakery, coated in flour and sugar and spice, lodging in a boardinghouse and saving my wages for a little place of my own. I aged—it was during these years that my hair began to gray, my eyes to fail, my skin to sag. Eventually I was able to buy a cottage—one that stood alone in the depths of the ancient forest. My new home was dark and rather drab, and on what seemed to me a whim, I decided to dress it up like one of my pastry creations. I ornamented it with *kekse* and bonbons, covered the wood siding in a façade of lebkuchen bricks mortared with white icing, coated the tar paper roof in hazelnut and almond shingles, constructed a picket fence of peppermint sticks. I lined the walkway with gargantuan gumdrops and replaced broken windowpanes with clear spun sugar. I made similar modifications to the interior—trimming the walls with a licorice chair rail, *platzchen* baseboards, and marzipan molding; tiling the kitchen with hard butterscotch; crafting furniture from *kipferln* and ribbon candy. I bought a colossal iron oven, one that took up a third of my kitchen, and started working from home, crafting my elaborate models on commission or carting them to the pastry shoppe to be displayed and sold.

I'd been in my little house for better than a year, oblivious to my deepening isolation, when on a crystalline autumn afternoon, I heard a strange sound—a scratching and scrambling. I thought squirrels or chipmunks were racing over the roof of my cottage, but when the sound persisted, then grew

louder, I hoisted myself up from the table—where I sat con-
structing a stollen and marzipan windmill—and stepped
onto the porch. Descending to the yard, I turned to glance up
at the roof. That was when I spied the boy.

He was perhaps ten years old with dark hair and large,
sunken eyes. He straddled the roof ridge, a brown ring
around his lips, a melting shingle gripped in each gooey hand.

"What do you think you're doing?" My voice creaked
with disuse.

"Don't be angry," the boy said. "I've only eaten four
shingles, and you have so many."

"Come down from there," I said. "It's dangerous. You
might fall."

Once he'd shimmied down a drainpipe, he offered me the
remains of the shingles. "I'm sorry," he said. "I haven't eaten
in days, and when I saw your house, I couldn't help myself."

I dismissed the shingles with a wave of my hand.
"Where are your parents?"

The boy dropped his head.

"Never mind," I said. "Come inside."

Yet another dearth lay upon the land, but living alone
with mountainous stores of flour, sugar, oil, salt, and spic-
es, I was only vaguely aware of this. I served the boy *rog-
genbrot* and pancakes, brötchen and pretzels, all of which
he devoured at a breakneck pace. The sounds he made—
the sighs and moans, the squeals of delight—pleased me,
and I piled pastries and baked goods upon his plate for
hours, until he thrust up a sticky hand.

"Please!" he cried, patting his swollen belly. "I cannot
eat another bite!"

We sat in my living room, sipping peppermint tea before
a crackling fire, as night wrapped its cold arms around the
forest. The boy, whose name was Dieter, sat close to me
on the sofa, his contented face and drowsy eyes giving the
impression of unwavering trust.

"So what's the story?" I asked. "Where are your parents?"

"Home with my seven brothers and sisters," he said,
"starving. I am the eldest boy, and I took it upon myself

to strike out in search of food. My father tried to stop me, but he was too weak. I've been wandering the forest for five days. When your cottage appeared, I thought surely I was fevered, but I touched the lebkuchen bricks and the *vanillekipferl* shutters and found them to be real. I wept with relief, for I knew whoever lived in such a house must love children."

While making the culinary modifications to my home, I hadn't once considered my unconscious motives, but I had to admit that the boy's interpretation had a singular logic. He maneuvered himself onto my lap, hung his arms around my neck, laid his head on my shoulder. I hadn't been so close to a child since Wilhelm, and I'd forgotten about their cottony smell. Sitting on the sofa, holding Dieter, I recalled how I'd wept as I ground Wilhelm between my teeth, as I watched his mother suck the marrow from his bones.

Dieter stayed with me for a month—sleeping in my bed, eating ten to twelve meals a day, helping me construct my pastry creations. It was midmorning, and we were working on an elaborate *baumkuchen* and *hutzelbrot* cathedral when he told me he wished to go home. He missed his family, he said. He'd been selfish, staying here with me and gorging on *pfeffernusse* and *süßigkeiten* while they starved. He wanted to cart a wheelbarrow full of baked goods back to his father's house. He begged me to save his parents and his siblings as I had saved him.

The boy stood opposite me at the kitchen table, affixing chocolate drops to the top of the *platzchen* wall surrounding the cathedral's courtyard. Directly behind him, the oven's glass door yawned open, ready to receive the flat sheets of dough I sat rolling out. Since he'd arrived, Dieter had put on weight, and my gaze roamed from his clothing—which now strained at the seams—to the taut skin of his face, and beyond him into the glowing interior of the oven.

"It has been a month," I said. "You cannot truly imagine that your family still lives."

He began to cry, his tears falling into the cathedral courtyard, but I was not yet finished.

"What would they think," I said, "if you came home
so fat and satisfied? Would they be able to forgive you?"

Dieter wept harder still. He wailed. He dropped his head
into his hands and tore at his hair. Blinded, he stumbled in
a circle, and when the open oven door struck his chubby
legs at the knee, he lost his footing and tumbled headlong
into its smoldering, gaping maw. He cried out, and the door
slammed—swallowing him—and I sat, as I had during the
entire episode, at the table rolling out *platzchen*, thinking of
how I would miss his small warmth in my bed, how I would
miss serving him cakes and bonbons, how I would miss fattening him. The desperate hunger that had driven me to partake of Wilhelm was a distant memory—I would eat Dieter
for entirely different reasons. I would lodge a piece of him
alongside his precursor, a piece that would comfort me until
another needy child ventured into the forest and stumbled
upon my edible cottage. It would be only a matter of time.

I have lost track of the years that have passed since that day,
of the countless children I have consumed—children driven
from their homes by famine, children I have filled to bursting,
children I can no longer distinguish from Wilhelm or Dieter.
By the time a fair-haired, apple-cheeked brother and sister
appear on my doorstep, I am almost as ancient as the forest
that embraces my cottage. My eyesight is nearly gone, and it
takes everything I have just to hobble onto the porch and say,
"Nibble, nibble, gnaw. Who is nibbling on my little house?"

They're older than most of the children who come to
me, and these siblings seem tougher, more jaded. They tell
me their father is a woodcutter, and I wonder if a reckoning
is upon me. Their mother died giving birth to the girl, and
they have been raised by a stepmother—a nasty woman.
Evil, they tell me. Wicked.

"She never loved us at all," says the girl.

"Not even one little bit," adds the boy. "She doesn't know
the first thing about being a mother."

They are even hungrier than their predecessors, these children of a woodcutter. They eat voraciously but are never satisfied, and it seems that I spend every moment standing in front of the oven, sliding in brötchen and pulling out *kletzenbrot*, making things with which to fatten them. Unlike the other children, they do not care to help me build my pastry structures, and I enter the kitchen one morning to find my masterpiece—a towering lebkuchen and *striezel* palace that rises from a mountaintop to disappear in the clouds, the kind of place I have decided people flock to in the afterlife, a model it has taken me weeks to craft—smashed beyond recognition. The boy blames the girl; the girl blames the boy, and they get into a fistfight, a brawl in which they toss one another around my cottage, shattering furniture and all of my extant creations—pfefferkuchen fortresses, *hutzelbrot* windmills, bridges made of stollen. I try to pry them apart, but I am too old, too weak, so I am forced to watch them until they run out of steam, until everything in my home has been decimated.

They do not sleep with me, this brother and sister, and in the dead of night, I hear them whispering—plotting from pallets on the floor. They want my edible house for themselves. They plan to take it and are just trying to decide how to get rid of me.

It will happen while I am standing at the oven. The girl will drop to the floor in front of me, and the boy will shove me from behind. Or maybe it will be the other way around; this is something they fight over—who gets to do the pushing. Once I have fallen headfirst into my colossal oven—once I am nestled amid the withering embers—they will slam shut the glass door and watch my hair sizzle, my skin crisp and peel and blacken. As they whisper in the night, they talk only of getting their hands on my house, of never having to go hungry again. They never mention why they would do such a thing to an old woman who has only given them food and shelter, but they do not need to. The instinct for self-preservation—as I may have already mentioned—is almost impossible to ignore.

As I stand now in front of the open oven door, reaching for a pan of fresh-baked lebkuchen and bracing myself for the push, my own instinct worn down by age and the weight of my transgressions, I think of this:

I bore our son—Albrecht's and mine—alone in the depths of the forest. Unwed, jilted, I hid my condition and disappeared, but living in the open, food was scarce, and I found myself starving. The child was born premature and still, covered in blood and fluids, his hands and feet perfection. I was nowhere near running water, so I licked him clean. I wrapped him in my only memento of my mother—the handmade lace shawl I wore on what should have been my wedding day—and with my bare hands, dug him a grave beneath the leaves that coated the forest floor. A pungent tang rose from the bottommost layer—an odor that never left my nostrils. I stretched out, supine, atop the grave and crossed my filthy hands over my chest, waiting for death, but I did not die. Hunger—the inexplicable need to preserve my own wretched life—eventually drove me to my feet. I wish that I had marked the spot, so I might at least have visited his tiny bones, or that I hadn't buried him at all, that I had eaten his flesh, which I am sure would have tasted sweeter than *striezel* or *kekse* or even *basler brunsli*—sweeter by far than anything else I have held upon my tongue.

# THE STORY WITHIN

*A*sphyxiation by corset didn't work, and neithe did the poisoned comb. In both instances the miniature men found her and were able to remove the offending object in time. You need an agent that is less obvious, a vehicle that will lodge deep inside her—a medium no one will be able to identify.

You have taken my suggestion, and a wilted version of you stands before me in the vaulted chamber. Furrows have carved a relief map into your taut skin. Your tongue darts between vacant gums to moisten desiccated lips. Opalescent cataracts bloom in the crystalline lenses of your eyes. Your finery has been replaced by burlap and rough wool, your crown by a knotted rag. From the crook of one arm hangs a basket of apples—it is out of this assortment that you will pluck the poisoned fruit.

"I am off then," you say.

I would nod, but I am inanimate, or mostly so. "Yes, O Queen."

"You are confident that this will work?"

"If she takes a bite of the apple, she will fall into eternal slumber."

"And she will never outshine me again?"

"Never is a long time," I say. "Especially when the story is still being written."

You step forward then, toward the wall on which I hang—east-facing as I have requested, so that I catch the first tendrils of morning light. You lift a hand, once white as snow, now braided with wine-dark veins, to brush my surface. You spread your palm open, splaying it upon the glass. This is not the first time you have asked how I came to abide in your mirror. In the past, I have refused to answer—not wishing to dredge up emotions I still possess despite my incorporeal state, not wishing to relive events that took place so long ago. I do not know if it is the thought of the poisoned fruit or of a girl imprisoned in slumber—or if it is simply the warmth of your skin—but on this occasion, I relent, and before I even collect my thoughts, words begin flowing from me like a mighty river. The dam is breached, and I know my tale will collect speed and force until there is no stopping it. We now have no choice but to duck our heads and ride it until it is done.

I have been told that I am the product of rape. That my father—a decorated soldier in the service of the Sultan—took one look at my fifteen-year-old gypsy mother, spirited her into a sheltered alley, snatched up her skirts, and forced his way inside her. I have been told that he was a man known for his even temperament and restraint. That after this brutal act, he returned to his tent, ate a light meal, prayed, and fell upon his scimitar. I have been told that my mother was killed when I was less than a year old by another soldier—one who spied her on a crowded street, went berserk, and tore her apart with his bare hands. "I had to see inside!" he is said to have cried as he was dragged away over the paving stones, his skin and uniform painted with her blood, his fingers still ripping at empty air. "I had to see how she was made!"

I have been told many things, but I am certain of only three. I grew up in opium dens, where my mother's brother and countless others tossed and moaned on piss-stained pallets in the pale fire of gas lamps, dreaming of truth or joy or beauty. From the time I was old enough to differentiate between types of men, I knew that I would someday wear tall, gleaming boots and carry a scimitar. And when I was twelve, an eye opened in the center of my chest—an eye that, until that time, had seemed nothing more than a harmless knot or fluid-filled cyst. I woke one morning into an eerie state of alertness, pricked by the sensation that something monumental was transpiring. I felt a strange tugging, pushed my thin blanket aside, and discovered the eye—equidistant from my nipples, now open and blinking, spinning in its socket, its lid-edges ragged, its lashes damp. I am not ashamed to admit that I screamed and ran to my uncle, who lifted his creased face from the pallet on which he lay, squinted at my chest, and nodded.

"The soldier who sired you had one, too," he said. "I wondered when it would open."

This eye was nothing like the eyes in my face, which were the color and shape of hazelnuts. It was much larger, and its hue swung wildly from palest blue to smoky gray. The eyeball itself seemed always to be moving—the pupil forever dilating and contracting—but it was not until I climbed into bed that first night that I began to understand something of its function. As soon as I shut the eyes in my head, I seemed to rise from my mat, to soar over cluttered, feculent streets, through the market stands and plazas of the Sultan's great city, over impregnable palace walls, beyond guards tense with readiness, hands on sword hilts, eyes stabbing deep into the night. I glided up a spiral staircase to the summit of a tower. The chamber I entered overflowed with varicolored cushions, carpets, and billowing draperies. Arched windows ushered in breezes collected from the cool desert night. Through the white netting that veiled a colossal bed, I spied a girl lying supine, a girl whose stillness indicated she was not merely sleeping—she was a prisoner of slumber. Everyone knew the story of the Sultan's daughter, who at seventeen had been fed a poisoned quince by one of her father's jealous wives and had slept, unchanged, for twelve years. Her remarkable face was unblemished, her ebony hair carefully braided around it, and in spite of my incorporeal state, the sight of her stole my breath. My third eye had sought her out the way a divining rod seeks aquiferous rock hidden beneath the scorched sands of the desert. Gazing at her made me feel at once whole and torn asunder, and I knew that it would not be possible, in my lifetime, for me to love another.

I became a man at sixteen, the day my mother's brother sucked for the last time on his clay pipe, lay back on his pallet, and let go of his soul. He was a great storyteller, my uncle, and I spent my boyhood listening to opium-fueled tales that spilled in a constant stream from his fissured lips. His bizarre narratives, which seamlessly melded disparate elements and eras, reminded me of gazing into a twisted mirror—one that not only reflects an object but also distorts it, so the resulting image mixes the familiar with the unexpected. Just before he died, he spoke to me of my mother—the irresistible innocent who drove men to madness—at some length. He told me she had cared for their father, also an addict, up until his end—force-feeding him, changing him, wiping shit from his backside and legs. When she was small, my uncle said, she loved nothing more than wallowing naked in burning desert sands. Her loveliness marked her more surely than a harelip or a club foot, setting her apart as an aberration, pushing her outside the realm of the natural. In the gloom of a windowless opium den, my uncle's voice began to trail away, and I knew that I would soon be alone in the world. A cold mantle of fear settled over me. I searched for his pupils, but they had vanished in the milky depths of his eyes. "What does it seek?" he asked, lightly touching my chest.

I covered his hand—a bone-and-tendon claw—with my own. "Beauty."

He seemed to smile, but I will never know if he heard my answer.

There was no money with which to bury my uncle, so his remains, like those of his father and my mother, were tossed into a debtor's grave. Afterward—following in the footsteps of the man from whose seed I had sprung—I enlisted in the service of the Sultan. I shined the boots of my superiors, silently taking their abuse, and in time found myself rising through the ranks. Eventually I was tapped to lead the Sultan's forces in an attack on a king whose holdings lay across the desert to the east. With my men, I set up camp in the shadow of a mountainous ridge of polychromatic dunes. We were to attack at first light, and alone in my tent, I unwrapped the bandage that hid the eye in my chest from view. I stretched out, eager to see the Sultan's sleeping daughter. In the eight years that had passed since I first found myself in her chamber, I had visited her nightly, and she had not changed—not her gown nor her hairstyle, not the position of her hands nor the angle of her chin. She was frozen outside time. Eternal. Part of me wanted her to wake, wanted to watch her thin, membranous lids flutter and open; part of me was so comforted by her constancy that I wanted her to go on sleeping forever.

I spent the night before the attack studying her. Having no idea which way the battle would go—whether the next day I would win a permanent place of leadership in the Sultan's service or lose my head and entrails to enemy forces—I found myself emboldened. Fearing that this might be the last time I would gaze upon the Sultan's daughter, I pushed through her white shroud. Though my body lay in a tent under a ridge of dunes miles away, though I had no hands or fingers, I was able to touch her. I caressed her slender arms, her angular shoulders. I stroked her cheeks, her forehead, her sloping nose. I slid up her skirts. She lay still as the tomb, but when I spread her legs, when I fondled her, her thighs seemed to quiver. Her chest seemed to heave. Her pelvis seemed to lift off the bed, thrusting upward of its own accord. I had been in the service of the Sultan four years, and like all soldiers had visited brothels, but whenever my turn came to lie down with one of the fading, fraying whores, I went flaccid. Now—relieved of the burden of my flesh—I did not have this problem, and I could come up with only one explanation: the Sultan's daughter loved me. I buried my face in her breasts and stomach, in her thighs and the dewy space between them. I crawled on top of her, seeking purchase and pleasure, and despite the fact that I had no form and she lacked animation, we came together in shocking, earth-quivering bliss.

The next day in battle I fought like one inhabited by demons. I plowed through the king's forces—a shimmering sea of conical helmets and hauberks, scimitars and sabers, lopping off heads and limbs like a man harvesting wheat. My mouth hung open in a roar, a ferocious cry filled with such lust for blood that the king's bravest soldiers fled before me. I had no pity for them, however, and chased them down to a man, slitting them open from clavicle to pubis, spitting on their remains.

Our attack was a rout, and my men celebrated by guzzling wine and tying slain enemies to their saddle horns, dragging the corpses over rough sands until they were no longer recognizable as human. As I drank with my men, the rage that had animated me during the battle receded, and I wondered what on earth had possessed me. I wanted glory—it was the only way an urchin such as myself would succeed—but I had, up to that point, imagined that in disposition I took after my uncle—the gentle taleteller. As I tried unsuccessfully to picture the men I had slain, fear encroached on my joy, and I was forced to admit that I had inherited more than the third eye of the brutish soldier who had forced himself upon my poor mother.

Though this tendency toward violence disconcerted me, it served me well. When our glorious Sultan heard of my victory, he set me at the head of a larger force and sent me after another king—one with even greater holdings. Once I destroyed that king's army and pilfered his treasures, the Sultan sent me after another king and another and another. His coffers swelled, and I was rewarded with a grand home adjacent to the palace, a home I filled with treasures—porcelain vessels and silk-embroidered tapestries, marble sculptures, enameled ornaments, furnishings inlaid with ivory and semi-precious stones—possessions of which, as a boy squatting beside my uncle, my head wreathed in opium smoke, I never would have dreamed.

I had few opportunities to enjoy my new wealth as I was forever campaigning; each time I defeated the forces of a king, the Sultan sent me to do battle with the armies of another. I grew accustomed to the nomadic life of a commander, to the camaraderie I shared with my men, and when we gathered at dusk to dine and drink and boast, I started entertaining them with tales my uncle had woven from the stinking pallets of my youth. The tricky wife who sneaks a lover into bed with her husband. The Sultan who takes a bear for his Grand Vizier. The ass who teaches a duck to swim. During the sixteen years I knew him, narratives erupted from my uncle in a constant stream, and I found at my disposal more stories than I could count. After taking leave of my men each night, I would retire to my tent, unbind my chest, close my eyes, and find myself transported to the chamber of the Sultan's sleeping daughter. I caressed her supple skin. I clambered on top of her and had my disembodied way with her. I imagined that we were falling in love. After a night of passionate yet formless intercourse, I would wake brimming with vigor and throw myself into the thick of battle, slaughtering in a haze, no longer aware of who or where or even what I was, possessed by a single goal—to destroy. To kill.

I had lost count of how many successive bloody victories I had won when I led my men back across the burning desert to the Sultan's great city. The gate swung open, and cheering crowds pelted us with scarves and sweets. They scattered rose petals beneath the hooves of our steeds. The wealth my men and I had gathered was evident—no fewer than six glittering temples were under construction, the streets were newly cobbled, and a gold statue of the Sultan towered before the palace. Inside, our glorious Sultan received me in his private chambers. He sat—colossal and rippling—swathed in robes of silk, cross-legged on a divan piled with cushions. Two muscular men fanned him with palm fronds while a youth tossed ripe dates into his large red mouth. The Sultan's eyes—buried in folds of sun-spotted flesh—sparked as I prostrated myself before him.

"Rise!" he cried, clapping his hands, and I sat back on my knees. He clapped again, and two men appeared carrying an ottoman, one they set at the foot of the divan. "Make yourself comfortable."

"Thank you, O Sultan," I said, touching my forehead to the carpets before settling on the ottoman.

"Tales of your exploits in battle continue to astound me," he said. "You have only to ask for something—anything over which I have command—and it is yours."

"Your daughter." The words fled my lips before I even realized they were forming. "I wish for her hand."

The Sultan's men stopped fanning. A date missed his mouth, damply pelting his voluminous cheek. The room was lit by a skylight cut into the vaulted ceiling, yet in spite of the radiance that drenched the chamber, clouds gathered in the Sultan's fleshy face. "What use is a wife who only slumbers?" he asked.

"I am not concerned with her usefulness, O Sultan."

Struggle was evident upon the features of our glorious Sultan. Before she had eaten the tainted quince, he had been devoted to his daughter. It was said that instead of eviscerating or beheading or banishing to the dungeons her poisoner—a clever woman who had once been his favorite wife—the Sultan had his sorcerers imprison her in a mirror, so that she could reflect beauty but would never again gaze upon her own.

"Surely you would rather have land," the Sultan said. "Spoils. My most nubile wife!"

I shook my head. "I am not of noble birth, but your people fall down before me in the streets. The coffers I have emptied in your service have made me a wealthy man. I will have no trouble caring for your daughter."

With a cry that mingled pain and anger, the Sultan pushed up from his divan. He stood over me, one trembling hand gripping the hilt of his scimitar. I would have prostrated myself had I not been wary of losing my head.

"My child!" he cried. "She deserves happiness! Yet she sleeps her life away!" He swayed on his swollen feet, his eyes locked on mine. After a pause that stretched like the boundless desert before a man who carries no water, he collapsed in front of the ottoman. Sobbing, he recounted the exploits of his young daughter—leaping from her bath to run, dripping suds, through the corridors of the palace; hiding every pair of boots he owned in an effort to prevent him from riding off to war; teaching his viziers to dance with veils. Gathering his ample body in my arms, I rocked our glorious Sultan, drying his cheeks, making soft sounds of comfort.

Shortly after the Sultan's daughter and I were pronounced man and wife, four guardsmen carried her from the tower in which she had slumbered for twenty years. Halfway down the winding staircase, one of the men dropped his corner of the litter, jolting the Sultan's daughter—rattling her like a ragdoll. The guards heard a cough, a retching, and the slap of an object colliding wetly with the stone wall. When the Sultan's daughter sat up, her brawny bearers shrieked and dropped the litter. They scrambled down the steps in a headlong rush, fleeing as though the girl had actually risen from the dead.

And in a way, she had. As it turned out, a fleshy bit of poisoned quince had been caught in her throat for two decades—a piece the clumsy guardsman had dislodged. Once the fruit was expectorated, her spell was broken. The Sultan's daughter was free. My fellow soldiers—men who had thought me mad—now pounded me on the back and pumped my hand. I accepted their congratulations, but as I watched the Sultan cover his daughter's face with kisses, explaining to her that he had allowed a commander in his service to marry her while she slumbered, I was aware only of her eyes. They were violet in hue, and from them, despondency flowed like a tide. It seemed that, for the Sultan's daughter, waking to find herself wed was more of a death sentence than twenty years under the influence of sleeping-poison had been.

The Sultan called his court to order. Viziers and councilors, wives and wine bearers, dancers and magicians, fire-eaters and sword-swallowers. Masters of the long-necked lute, the end-blown flute, the violin, the plucked zither, and the kudum drum. A celebration of his daughter's awakening and marriage was soon underway, one that erupted from the palace into the sun-drenched streets of the city and beyond—into the vast stillness of the desert. At a lapis-inlaid marble table, the Sultan placed his daughter on one side of him and me on the other, but even when I could no longer see her eyes, I sensed her hopelessness—her unequivocal anguish. Too late, I realized our love had been nothing more than a fantasy, and even before my wife and I had a proper conversation, I feared that I had made a dreadful mistake.

The profound sadness of the Sultan's daughter tainted the air in my home, making it difficult for me to breathe. Though her twenty-year slumber had robbed her of the ability to sleep, she rarely rose from bed, languishing throughout the day and night, shivering and weeping or simply staring, her eyes fixed on a point to which I had no access. Her bones ached, she said, and every strand of hair on her head hurt, yet the Sultan's physicians could find nothing wrong. Her symptoms were identical to those that had plagued my uncle when he was deprived of opium, and I could not help but wonder if the sudden removal of the sleeping-poison from my wife's bloodstream was to blame for her discomfort. Kneeling beside her plush couch as I had once knelt beside my uncle's pallet, I remembered how his tales had comforted me—distracting me from the meanness of our existence—and I told them to the Sultan's daughter. The tale of the princess who gives birth to a goat, and the tale of twin brothers who share a wife without her knowledge. The tale of the gluttonous Sultan who puts to death any man who can best him in a footrace, and the tale of the innkeeper with the hindquarters of a camel. The tale of the third son of the Sultan.

"When he was still a boy," I said, "the Sultan's third son realized that after his older brothers plundered their father's holdings, he would be left with nothing, so he ran away from the Sultanate to learn the art of war. He traveled widely—soldiering for a number of kings—until he found himself back in his homeland, fighting in the service of his father. He fought well and bravely—rising through the ranks, winning countless battles, amassing a small fortune for himself and a larger fortune for the Sultanate. When he first laid eyes upon the Sultan's only daughter, the third son of the Sultan felt as though he'd been struck by an errant bolt of desert lightning. The girl had not yet been born when he left home, but she was now a matchless beauty, and though the third son of the Sultan knew it was wrong, he loved her."

As I spoke, dawn spilled over the Sultan's great city, and my wife grew still. She stopped weeping. She stopped shivering. By the time I finished my story, she sat bolt upright. For the first time since she had woken, her violet eyes were full of something other than despair. They were full of curiosity. Of wonder.

"Who told you these tales?" she said.

"The uncle who raised me."

"Some are tales my old nurse used to send me off to sleep with," she said, "but not this one. Not the tale of the third son of the Sultan. Tell me, who was your uncle?"

"A man of no consequence," I said, guilt stabbing me in the throat.

The Sultan's daughter crawled across the mattress. She wore a white gown, and her hair flowed in a loose curtain around her. Strengthening light pushed into the room. I could see the shape of her body through her gown, and I was flooded with desire. She stopped in front of me, her violet eyes plumbing mine. "Who is your father?"

"I have been told that he was a soldier in the Sultan's service."

"He no longer lives?"

"I have been told that he took his own life."

"And your mother?"

"I have been told that she was murdered."

My wife reached out, lightly touching my chest. Beneath my coat, I felt my third eye blink and spin.

"You think me beautiful," she said.

"I have never seen another who can compare."

She sighed, and sorrow crept back into her violet eyes. "You will."

I assured her that I would not.

"Beauty is fleeting," she said, "and men cannot help but chase it. That is why my father keeps marrying. When he wed my mother, she was the fairest maid within a thousand miles, but she was vain. She sat staring into a looking glass for hours, searching for imperfections. Growing up, I thought this was what it was to be a woman, and I sat beside her with my own small mirror. I stifled smiles and laughter to prevent wrinkling. Morning and night, I rubbed salves and creams into my skin. I used kohl and various pigments to enhance my features. When I was ten, the Sultan's youngest wife—the woman people had been saying outshone even my mother— was poisoned, and my mother was accused. Rather than face the wrath of our glorious Sultan, she decided to end her life. She took me for a walk in the palace gardens. In front of a dancing fountain, she knelt and took my shoulders. She did not say she loved me—she told me to take care of my face. She assured me that she was innocent of the murder, but I did not know whether to believe her. I still do not know."

As she finished her tale, the Sultan's daughter rose for the first time in days. She tried to cross the room but wobbled so wildly that had I not caught her, she would have crashed to the carpets. She felt weightless in my arms, and I carried her to her dressing table. I deposited her upon the bench, and she sat with her elbows propped on the counter, studying her face.

"It was for the best," she said. "My mother could not have faced growing old, and she did not equip me for it."

"But you have not changed since the day you fell into your slumber."

"I am not the same," she said, shaking her head. "I never should have woken."

My wife was just beginning to recover from the lingering effects of the sleeping-poison when her father once again sent me off to war. I regretted leaving the Sultan's daughter, but I soon recalled the pleasure I took in pounding over scorched desert sands, in gathering with my men each night to drink and tell tales. We traveled hundreds of miles to battle the forces of a second Sultan, and the evening before the attack, we set up camp beneath towering kaleidoscopic dunes. When I stretched out in my tent and lowered my lids, my third eye instantly closed the distance it had taken us a fortnight to travel, and I found myself in my wife's chamber. For the first time since she had woken from her twenty-year slumber, she appeared to be sleeping. The sight aroused me. I reached out to massage her skin, and she seemed to lift her hips, to open herself—to invite me inside. I slid up her skirts and clambered atop her, stiff and swollen with what still felt to me like love.

We engaged the second Sultan's forces at dawn, and I solitarily dispatched some two hundred soldiers. Several I tore to pieces with my bare hands. Surrounded by the ragged, gory remnants of men, I dropped to my knees beside a legless enemy commander. As he moaned feverishly—whispering in a language I could not understand—I thrust my hand into his perforated chest, seized his still-pumping heart, and tore it free of its moorings. Lifting it to my lips, I devoured the fist-sized muscle in three colossal bites. My own men—some of the most sanguinary soldiers ever to carry a scimitar—turned away from the sight. A few of them vomited. The commander's blood ran hot and metallic down my throat and cascaded from my unshaven chin. As my urgent desire to stamp out life slowly receded, I saw myself as I must have appeared to the men I faced in battle, and I was horrified. What would my uncle think of what I had become? Had the poor gypsy who bore me realized she had spawned a monster?

After bathing and changing, I entered the palace of the second Sultan to negotiate the terms of his surrender. In his chambers, the second Sultan—a tall, jagged man—sat stiffly upon a divan. To his left sat a young girl, and the sight of her almost made me lose my footing. Her limbs were slender, her pink lips plump, her hair like spun copper, her eyes the aquamarine of the pools in a certain oasis. From an objective standpoint, her beauty thrust that of my wife into the shadows, and I wondered how it was that the eye in my chest had not carried me to this incomparable girl the night before.

"So you are the butcher," said the second Sultan.

I stood at rigid attention. "Your forces have been vanquished," I said, pulling a scroll of parchment from my coat. "If you sign your holdings over to my glorious Sultan, I will spare your life."

"To wander the desert as a pauper?" said the second Sultan. The girl placed a hand on his bony shoulder, but he shrugged her away. "I would rather die than see my Sultanate in the hands of some fat foreigner."

"Father," the girl said, but the second Sultan lifted a finger to silence her.

"It is your choice," I said, unsheathing my scimitar. "If you prefer to die, so be it."

The second Sultan rose. He approached me, smiling grimly. "What pleasure do you take in killing?"

"I am merely a soldier serving my glorious Sultan."

"You are a butcher," said the second Sultan, and he spat in my face. "A soldier kills with honor. There is no honor in eating a man's still-beating heart."

His mouth twitched; his eyes glinted wetly. His spittle dripped from my nose, but I did not feel fury. I was instead filled with pity. "Here," I said, thrusting the parchment at him. "Sign this, and I will let you live."

The second Sultan looked like he wanted to shred the scroll, but he glanced at the copper-haired girl. "I have sired five sons and a daughter," he said. "One boy did not live to adulthood, and today you massacred the rest of my male heirs. If I do not sign, what will become of my daughter?"

"Lest her future sons swear vengeance on my glorious Sultan," I said, showing no sign of the regret that filled me at this thought, "she will be put to death."

"And if I sign?"

I glanced at the girl, whose lovely face had shattered. "My Sultan is always looking for wives."

The second Sultan made a strangled sound. He shuffled to a gilded table, where he unrolled the parchment and scratched his signature into the bottom. He asked for a moment alone, and I nodded. His daughter launched herself at him; he wound his arms around her, burying his face in her shining hair. He then ducked behind an elaborately embroidered curtain. The girl attempted to flay the flesh from my bones with her aquamarine gaze, and I looked away. A moment later, we heard a heavy thud, and I shoved aside the curtain to find that the second Sultan had fallen upon his scimitar.

I did not feel that I could trust my men with the second Sultan's daughter, so she traveled across the sands on my saddle before me. In the beginning she refused to speak or drink from my canteen. I pitched a tent for her beside my own at night—tying one end of a silken rope around her wrists and the other around my waist, tethering us one to the other—but the sound of her weeping plagued me, making it impossible for me to sleep. On those nights in the desert, my third eye showed me only my slumbering wife; I was never transported into the tent of the second Sultan's daughter.

Halfway through the journey, she began relating to me a story—an account of a thin Sultan defeated by the forces of a fat Sultan. The fat Sultan's cruel commander butchered the thin Sultan and his four sons, but he carried the thin Sultan's daughter off to become one of the fat Sultan's wives. She was a clever girl, however, and she managed to escape into the desert, where she plotted revenge against those who had crushed her family. When they least expected it, she materialized out of vaporous air to separate the fat Sultan's head from his corpulent frame. But the commander who had eaten her favorite brother's heart on the field of battle did not get off so lightly. She eviscerated him—drawing out his intestines inch by inch. She then wound them around his throat, strangling him until he was dead.

Three days before we reached the great city of my glorious Sultan, we stopped to water the horses at a certain oasis with clear aquamarine pools, and the second Sultan's daughter vanished. Her hands and feet were bound, but search as we might, my men and I could find no trace of her. It was as if she had sunk beneath the scorching sands, or been carried away on a hot gust of wind. I knew she could not survive alone in the desert, and as we rode on, I scanned the horizon for her proud, pleasing figure. Tears leaked from my eyes for the first time since my uncle had drawn his last rattling breath.

When I returned to my home, I found my wife much improved. She was no longer in such pain and now slept through the night. While I was away, she had rearranged my ornaments and furnishings and had brought in treasures from her father's palace. She glided around in the embroidered gowns of a Sultana—her hair unerringly arranged, her face decorated with ground malachite, ochre, and kohl. In slumber she had seemed younger, softer, and more yielding. Awake, her general bearing—the way she carried herself and the ease with which she handled our servants—revealed her imperial upbringing, and I began to notice how comfortable she was wielding power.

She smiled and even laughed now—but in certain light, I saw lingering traces of the desolation that had flowed from her when she first woke from her twenty-year slumber. I would come upon her sitting before a dancing fountain in the palace gardens, and before she could compose her features, despair would leak from her violet eyes. This vestigial sorrow and the memory of my inability to perform with the whores I had visited in the past conspired to prevent me from venturing into my wife's chamber at night. The fact that our union had never been officially—or indeed, physically—consummated was something of which we never spoke.

At this time our glorious Sultan's heart began to fail. He was no longer a young man and was not expected to sire more children. Of his three sons, one had run off and the other two had been killed in battle. On a particularly sultry night, the Sultan hosted a banquet at which he announced that upon his death, control of the Sultanate would pass to his daughter. My wife received this news with a gracious smile. After the meal she suggested that I entertain the assembly with an anecdote, and I obliged—telling the story of the princess who dresses as a man in order to ride into battle with her brothers, and who proves to be the deadliest of her siblings. Once the applause of the viziers and wives and councilors and hangers-on died down, the Sultan's daughter announced that she, too, wished to tell a tale. "It is the tale of the third son of the Sultan," said she.

"There was once a powerful Sultan who sired three sons and a daughter. When each of his children reached the age of twelve, an eye opened in the center of his or her chest—an eye whose hue varied from lightest blue to smoky gray, an eye forever blinking and spinning in its socket. The Sultan himself had no such eye, nor had any of his wives, but he had heard of such all-knowing orbs, and he believed they revealed the heart's greatest desire. The first and second sons of the Sultan lusted for fortune and dominion, so their third eyes revealed to them the hidden riches of other kings and Sultans. Their father sent his armies against these rulers, and his soldiers exterminated thousands, and his holdings multiplied, and he grew fat and obscenely wealthy."

My wife paused, and I peered down the long table at our glorious Sultan, who lounged on a divan with two of his most nubile wives. As his daughter spun her tale, he sat up and pushed aside his wives. His moon-shaped face began to pale.

"The third eye of the Sultan's third son," my wife continued, "did not show him hoarded treasure. It showed him

a girl—the loveliest he had ever seen. When he revealed
this to his father and brothers, they laughed, mocking him
because he was not desirous of power and assets above
all things. He could turn only to his sister—the youngest
of the Sultan's children and the one with whom he had
always been closest. Eventually, bruised by the ridicule of
his father and brothers, the sensitive third son of the Sultan left home in search of the captivating girl he had seen
only with his third eye."

A murmur filled the banquet hall, and color continued
to drain from our glorious Sultan. Sweat streaked his face,
darkening his robes. His wives tried to mop his brow, but he
shooed them away. One of his hands grasped convulsively
at the center of his chest.

"The Sultan's third son traveled the desert," my wife
continued, "soldiering in the service of various rulers, but
it was not until he returned to his home—to the great city
of his father—that he found her. Walking the crowded
streets in his uniform, he spotted a gypsy girl of unrivaled
beauty—one who glided over the cobbled streets and
darted through the crush of bodies like a fish. He followed,
finally reaching out to touch her shoulder, to tell her he
had been searching for her, that he loved her. But as his
fingers brushed her skin, he was filled with a savage lust
he had never before known, and he found himself pushing
the girl into a deserted alley, where he shoved her against
a wall and took her by force."

Our glorious Sultan attempted to rise, but he collapsed
onto his divan. The assembly did not move to help him—
they sat mesmerized by the tale of his daughter, who had
not yet finished.

"Horrified by what he had done, the third son of the Sultan sought out his sister and confessed his crime. He was
devastated to learn that his heart's desire could be twisted into something so ugly, and he blamed his third eye for
bringing out brutal tendencies he never knew he harbored.
He told his sister he could not live with himself, and though
she tried to stop him, he broke away and ran into the palace

gardens. Before his favorite fountain, he fell upon his scimitar. When the Sultan learned what had transpired, he had the incident—and his third son—buried anonymously. The Sultan's daughter was the only person ever to visit her brother's grave. Afterward, she ate a ripe quince filled with poison."

"It is not true!" cried our glorious, gasping Sultan. His face went white as marble as he clutched at his chest. "Your brother ran away when he was a boy! He was never heard from again! My jealous wife gave you the poisoned quince!"

Hurrying to her father's side, my wife knelt to stroke his pallid face. The floor of the banquet hall—whose mosaic tiles depicted a younger, thinner Sultan standing in a field of poppies, surrounded by his children—seemed to heave like the deck of a sailing ship, and I found myself clinging to the table for dear life. "I do not understand this reaction," said the Sultan's daughter, her violet eyes skewering me where I sat, unable to move. "It was nothing more than a tale."

My wife and I never spoke of my father or her brother—the Sultan's third son—and whether they were one and the same. But our union was never consummated, and as soon as she was named Sultana, she took another husband and another and another. Each was younger and more handsome than the last; these were the husbands who lay with her—and planted the seeds of heirs inside her.

I never saw the eye in her chest, but I am convinced that she had one, and I never learned what it revealed to her—the Sultana did not make me privy to her heart's desire. For a time I thought it must have shown her the Sultan's third son—for whom she bore an unnatural desire—and after he died, it showed her nothing but a bitter void. Or perhaps, once her brother was gone, her third eye sought out the son of the Sultan's third son. Perhaps during her twenty-year slumber, she watched me sitting beside my uncle in the opium dens of my youth. Perhaps she heard the tales he told. Perhaps she saw me slaughtering thousands in the name of her father. Perhaps she witnessed my disembodied defilement of her own flesh.

I decided that the Sultana took after her father
͏nd second sons. That *power* was what she
͏ll. That the Sultan's third son was the only
͏ıs siblings whose third eye had shown him something
*other* than secreted wealth. The Sultana sent her armies out
in even greater force than her father had. She encouraged
their bloodlust and savagery, and she swelled her coffers to
bursting, and under her long rule, the Sultanate's holdings
increased tenfold. One of the Sultan's nubile wives—the only
person ever to suggest that she told her tale that night in the
banquet hall for the express purpose of stopping her father's
massive heart—was impaled on an iron spike atop the palace wall.

After our Sultan's inglorious demise, I tried to continue
soldiering for the Sultanate, but I had lost my vicious edge.
I could no longer plow through a horde of enemy troops—
swinging my scimitar, executing with abandon. The butcher who had once eaten a man's still-beating heart was no
more. Moreover, my third eye continued carrying me from
a tent pitched alongside the field of battle to the bedside
of the Sultana, but I had lost my desire to push up her
skirts and clamber on top of her. I had become as impotent
without my body as I had always been while imprisoned
within it.

Deprived of the camaraderie of my men, I tried befriend-
ing the Sultana's other husbands. I sat with them around
the communal table at which they took their meals—sharing my tales—but they did not care to listen, and I found
their inane chatter and obsession with appearance intoler-
able. I spent most of my time wandering the palace and
gardens alone, acutely aware of my own uselessness. As I
grew increasingly isolated, I was consumed by thoughts of
my dear departed uncle and my poor gypsy mother and the
Sultan's ill-fated third son—a man destroyed by the empty
promises of beauty. Before a dancing fountain in the palace
gardens, I was assaulted by visions of a soldier who shared
my face falling upon his scimitar—blood leaking from his
chest to feed the roots of citron shrubs and cypress trees.

Finally, I decided to approach the Sultana and ask her to dissolve our marriage bond. She reclined—as her father had—on a divan in her chambers. By this time she had borne two sons and two daughters. Her age was showing, but she was still radiant. I prostrated myself before her, pressing my face into the carpets spread there, and begged her for release.

"Rise!" She clapped her hands, and I sat back on my knees. "If I grant your request, where will you go?"

I had no skill or ambition, no family or friends. There was only one place for me, and I looked forward to stretching out on piss-stained pallets in the opium dens of my youth. I recalled how my uncle's face had changed when the smoke flooded his brain—the joy that wipes away age and cares and the shadows that loom always around us. I had been dreaming for some time of the freedom such an existence would afford me, but as I knelt before the Sultana, I knew it would continue to hover outside my grasp. Even if she agreed to release me, the bond we shared ran deeper than the ties of matrimony, and it had—thus far— proved to be unbreakable.

"You woke me from my slumber," the Sultana said, making a gesture with both hands—a sign that seemed to encompass the palace, the Sultanate, the entire world. "All of this is your doing."

My third eye was not, as I once believed, a divining rod in search of an abstract concept such as truth or joy or beauty. It was not, as our glorious Sultan had understood, an orb capable of reaching into the human heart and sifting through the detritus there to find one's greatest desire. It was an agent of enslavement—permanently tethering its host to some particular person, place, or thing. This might be called *love*, but it would probably better be termed *obsession*. Regardless, my eye could show me only the Sultana for as long as she lived, and if I wanted to while away the rest of my days in an opium slumber, I would dream of nothing but her.

I see now that I should have bided my time—I should have devised a clever scheme, or snuck up on the Sultana ιle she toured the palace gardens alone, or poured finely ground glass into her baba ghanoush. But as she made that all-inclusive gesture—as she reclined on her divan and confirmed for me the nagging fear that I was the author of my own destiny—the wanton lust for destruction that had once animated me in battle stirred within me. I found myself rising, drawing my scimitar, charging the Sultana with a mighty cry. Her guardsmen ringed the chamber, and they stopped me with ease. My wife nodded, and the guards balled their fists. The room reverberated with the thud of their blows to my face and body, with the grunts and cries that escaped me, with the crackle and snap of my bones. Even as strange clouds bloomed in my vision, I thought I recognized some of my attackers as men who had served under me when I led the forces of our glorious Sultan against the first king I ever defeated. I tried to speak—to remind them of our bloody rout, of the victory we had shared—but their fists rained so heavily upon my mouth that I could not open it.

"Enough!" the Sultana finally cried, and when her guards no longer supported me, I collapsed like boiled eggplant on the carpets. My coat had been torn open, and though I could not lift my head, I knew that for the first time since I had shown it to my uncle at twelve years old, my third eye was exposed. I felt it blink and spin; I was aware of the dilation and contraction of its pupil. The murmurs of the guardsmen— some of wonder, some of disgust—swelled as the Sultana swam into my line of vision. Kneeling, she trained her violet gaze on my chest, and for a moment, the heavenly motions of the stars that pocked the deep desert nights ground to a halt. Confronted with the object it had previously viewed only through a veil of space and time, my third eye did something it had never done before. It wept—voluminous, salty droplets that cascaded over my nipples and down my abdomen. The pain that accompanied these tears was far worse than the beating I had suffered at the hands of the Sultana's guards- men, and if I hadn't lost consciousness, I would have begged them for another round.

For my attempt on her life, the Sultana had her sorcerers imprison me in this mirror. I spent much of my time fuming and railing against injustice in the beginning, but eventually I grew accustomed to my prison. In corporeal form I had wrought only death and destruction, and once I was able to admit this, I was relieved to be quit of the cumbersome burden of my flesh. I believe the Sultana thought it especially cruel to hang me in her chamber—to force me constantly to reflect her image—but over the years, she forgot that my position was a punishment. As she aged, her vanity burgeoned—eclipsing her other shortcomings—and she sat before me for hours searching her face for imperfections, just as her mother had, chattering about her looks, about how she had once been the fairest maid within a thousand miles. In time I became her closest companion, her confidant—the only one she felt she could trust.

But she was sorely mistaken.

I had been hanging on the Sultana's wall for many years when a slender, black-clad figure entered her chamber in the dead of night. I could have woken the Sultana with a cry, but I did not. In the moon's anemic light, I watched the proud figure hoist a glinting scimitar and bring it down, separating the Sultana's head from her body. Though I have no proof, I like to think that the assassin was the beautiful daughter of the second Sultan—the girl with copper hair and aquamarine eyes, the girl who swore revenge for the ruin of her family. For years after she vanished at the oasis, I would wake in the night, my body tense, listening for her stealthy footsteps, wondering if she could have survived the desert, if she would make good on her threat to strangle me with my intestines. In my mind I expanded on the tale she told me—embellishing here and padding there—and over time, I built the second Sultan's daughter up into a heroine, one devoted to avenging those who have been dealt with unjustly. It is only fitting then, that in the tale I have writ, she should be the one to finally release me from my enslavement to the Sultana. That she should reenter the narrative—better late than never—to clip the tether and allow my third eye to turn away from the object of its obsession—to become all-knowing at last.

When I started my story, night still blacked the mullioned windows of your castle, but now that I have finished, the sun dangles like a paper disk over the surrounding wood. I left the desert centuries ago—or rather, I was stolen away—but I have never become acclimated to how feebly that sovereign star illuminates this part of the world.

You have dropped your basket, and apples have scattered, rolling around the room. Some have disappeared beneath the four-poster bed, others beneath the dresser and armoire, but you seem not to have noticed. Tears glisten in the furrows and folds of the face you wear—the glamour that obscures your beauty—and I am taken aback by the sight.

"That is quite a story," you say.

"It is longer than I remembered."

"What became of you after the death of the Sultana?"

"I hung in the palace until the forces of her son were conquered by an invading army. I was then removed to the sleeping chamber of another Sultan's wives. I remained there for years, until that Sultanate was also overtaken. I have been sold, stolen, and presented as a gift. I have changed hands countless times—the telling of those events would take close to an eternity."

You stand peering into my frame, and I know you are trying to make out something beyond your reflection. To catch a glimpse of me.

"How did it feel?" you ask.

"How did what feel?"

"Being released from the Sultana," you say. "Being set free."

In the thirty years that I have hung on the wall of your chamber, I have recounted for you thousands of tales, and you have asked me for daily affirmation of your beauty, but we have never before spoken of feelings, and it occurs to me that my story has irrevocably changed things between us.

"I was miserable," I say, surprising myself. "She was my true north. To this day, I miss her."

You had planned to strike out at first light, but listening to my tale has put you behind schedule. You now scurry around on all fours, retrieving apples. Once the red fruits are nestled in your basket, you study them, trying to determine which one is tainted.

As usual, I see all—past, future, naked children kneeling in squalor on cobbled streets, the ripple that will mature into a tidal wave, black poison pulsing beneath the skin of the apple in your right hand. You have decided this one is safe, and you are hungry. As I watch you lift the blighted fruit to your mouth, I recall the peace that reigned over the Sultana's countenance when she was a prisoner of slumber. I have seen your end, and I know it will not be quick or easy. You will not be killed by an assassin in your bed. The girl you are about to poison will not sleep eternally. She will wake and marry a prince. At her wedding you will be forced to don red-hot iron shoes and dance until you fall down dead. If I let you eat the poisoned apple, you will be spared this pain and humiliation. You will be released from the vain obsession that rules your life. I can rewrite your story, and for a moment, I consider doing so.

"Be careful, O Queen," I say instead. "That is the poisoned fruit."

I do not want you to suffer, but I find that I am unwilling to let you go. Through arched windows, I watch you hobble over a flagstone path that rings your castle. You vanish into a cluster of trees—larch and yew, hornbeam and white willow, black poplar and silver birch—and I will not relax until you reappear in the same spot. Of all those who have studied their reflections in my surface—of those who have revealed to me some facet they have never shown another—you are the first to whom I have told my story. I can no longer verify its utter veracity, but it is all I have, and entrusting it to you has shown me that it is not yet complete. It lacks one of the elements no good tale can survive without—an ending.

Perhaps the future I have seen is pure fiction. Perhaps the seven bantam men will bury the girl, and the prince will never find her. Or her coffin will not be jostled hard enough to dislodge the poisoned fruit. Or she will wake, but she will find it in her ample heart to forgive you. She will convince her husband to forgo the iron shoes, and she will instead toss the bouquet in your direction. Seat you at her right hand at the reception. Her generosity will touch you—convincing you to become a different kind of person. It could happen. After all, this tale is still being written. You will find a way to release me from your mirror. We will flee this bitter clime and take up residence in an opium den half a world away. Stretched out side-by-side on piss-stained pallets, we will spend our remaining days sunk into the blessed stupor of ever after.

## ACKNOWLEDGMENTS

This book was my MFA thesis project. Before beginning each story, I first reread and studied the text(s) that inspired it. For each piece, I endeavored to find a brand-new access-point into a well-known tale; over time, I have come to see that this is how every piece of writing works.

I want to thank the kind folks at Hollins Univerity who read these stories in their inchoate stages and gave me invaluable feedback: Rase McCray, Ashley Good, Laura Conrad, Cathy Hankla, and especially Jeanne Larsen. I also want to thank the writers Heather Newton and Maggie Marshall, who kindly read early drafts of the book. It was Heather who suggested the book's title.

In addition, I wish to pay homage to Dr. George Stade—former Professor Emeritus of English Literature at Columbia University. Professor Stade's "Forms of Popular Fiction" course introduced me to not only some of the tales I retell in this book, but also the notion that "high" art and "low" art are far more aligned than we may assume—a notion that echoes throughout this book, and indeed all my work.

Big thanks to my family members, supporters, and friends—especially my husband, Bill Gatewood. For these stories I must also thank Scheherazade, Homer, the Brothers Grimm, Daphne du Maurier, Sir Arthur Conan Doyle, Hermes, William Shakespeare, J.M. Barrie, Rudyard Kipling, Herman Melville, Vladimir Nabokov, Italo Calvino, Jorge Luis Borges, and Angela Carter.

Jen Fawkes is the author of *Mannequin and Wife: Stories* (2020, LSU Press). Her work has appeared in *One Story, Lit Hub, Crazyhorse, The Iowa Review, Joyland, The Rumpus, Best Small Fictions 2020*, and many other venues. Her fiction has won numerous prizes, from *The Pinch, Salamander, Harpur Palate, Washington Square Review*, and others. She lives in Little Rock, Arkansas, with her husband and several imaginary friends.

CPSIA information can be obtained
at www.ICGtesting.com
Printed in the USA
BVHW031014070321
601770BV00009B/17